Blissfully Undone

 Red Phoenix

SIGN UP FOR MY NEWSLETTER
HERE FOR THE LATEST RED
PHOENIX UPDATES

SALES, GIVEAWAYS, NEW
RELEASES, PREORDER LINKS,
AND MORE!
SIGN UP HERE
REDPHOENIXAUTHOR.COM/
NEWSLETTER-SIGNUP

CONTENTS

Blissfully Snowbound

J enny grabbed her luggage and threw it in Dan's car, her hair whipping crazily from a sudden blast of chilling wind. "So where is Kelly? I thought she was going to help us get the cabin ready."

Dan smiled uneasily. "Well, you know Kelly. Said she was running late and would meet us up there."

She snorted in disgust as she got into his car. "I don't know how you put up with that woman." Although Kelly was her best friend, Jenny resented how she always seemed to 'run late' when work needed to be done.

"So where is Ryan?" Dan asked with a smirk, as he drove them to the discount supermarket.

"Oh, Mr. Workaholic had just one more meeting. So you know what that means…"

"Yep, we get to run all the errands before we head up."

"And I really *hate* grocery shopping," Jenny

complained. "I suggest we only buy things we like. Screw those two!"

Dan laughed. "Why not? Let's go all out."

Jenny loved the ease she felt around Dan. The four of them were that perfect combination of friends. The couples had met in college three years ago, and still hung out together. Kelly and Dan were nicknamed the Blondies for obvious reasons, and Jenny was part of the Brownhead team. Jenny had some Cherokee blood running in her veins from her dad's side. It gave her an exotic look with her long, dark hair and soft, brown eyes. Ryan was her perfect match because of his chocolate-brown curls— everyone said so.

Jenny appreciated how rare it was that Kelly's boyfriend was best friends with her boyfriend. It made trips like this a ton more fun. The four pretty much did everything together, including vacations to Jamaica and Hawaii. This weekend it was Dan's family cabin up in the mountains.

"I've got a suggestion," Dan said. "Since you and I hate to cook, let's just buy convenience foods. You know, all that premade crap that Kelly and Ryan hate."

She chuckled. "Oh, I like the way you think!" she said as she grabbed a shopping cart and headed inside.

The two of them were sinful the way they filled up the cart with chemically enhanced foods. She knew Ryan was going to have a cow, but he deserved it.

Dan threw in some marshmallows, chocolate, and graham crackers. Jenny patted his shoulder enthusiastically. "Yay! I've never had s'mores before."

"Wow. I didn't appreciate what a sheltered life you've led, Jenny. How else can I corrupt you this weekend?"

She grinned, looking down the row of food. "I've never had Vienna sausages."

"Done." Dan threw six cans of the little sausages into the cart.

The snow was starting to accumulate on the roads by the time they finished packing their stock of liquor into the car. "Plenty of food and booze, I think we're set. I sure hope they get on the road soon. It is going to ice up fast," Jenny fretted.

"Don't worry. Kelly promised to leave by four. What about Ryan?"

"He's not leaving the meeting until five. He'll be driving in the dark by the time he gets there."

"Maybe you should call him and suggest a quicker exit."

Jenny called his cell, but Ryan didn't pick up. She left a message and then another one at his office. "That's the best I can do. Hope he listens to it in time."

Dan started his car and grinned at her. "I know Ryan. A blinking light at his desk will drive him crazy. He'll get your message."

The drive up proved to be more difficult than they expected. The mountains had at least ten inches of snow and the flakes were still falling with a vengeance. "You want to turn back?" Jenny asked.

"No, we're almost there. The weathermen said it should be a quick storm. I'm sure it'll clear up some before they get here."

They arrived at Dan's cabin after four. The sky was dark and heavy with snow. It didn't appear to Jenny that it was stopping anytime soon. "Dan, we better get a fire going first thing. I can just imagine Kelly's agitated state after driving up. Nothing calms her more than a warm fire."

He nodded in agreement. "I'll grab some firewood after we get the supplies in."

While Dan took care of the wood, Jenny ripped off the covers from the furniture and loaded the dishwasher. Experience from past trips had taught her that the dishes needed a quick wash to get rid of the taste of disuse. Then she went about making the beds.

Dan came in with a huge armful of wood. "I'll get more in the morning, but this should be plenty for the night. Thank goodness we have power! I can't imagine how cold this place would get without it, especially with the wind starting to pick up. Kelly and Ryan better get here soon."

Jenny glanced nervously at the clock. "Do you think they're all right?"

Dan's smile was reassuring. "Don't worry. Both Kelly and Ryan are capable drivers. They'll be here within the hour, I'm sure of it."

The two snacked on Doritos and Vienna sausages while they waited. Dan had a pleasant fire going and Jenny put rocking tunes on. Both of them were Blue October fans, so she decided to indulge in the emotionally potent lyrics as they munched.

Dan sighed when *Congratulations* came on. "This song always makes me sad."

"It is a sad song, isn't it? Justin must have really loved the girl."

"Yeah."

"I enjoy the angst in his songs, don't you?" Jenny said, thrilled to share her enthusiasm for the music. Ryan never listened to lyrics—they weren't his thing. "Justin's work is so real and raw."

He agreed. "The man definitely puts his soul out for public consumption."

"I wish more singers were open and real like that."

Dan cleared his throat and said, "It takes guts to put your feelings on the table."

Jenny jumped on his comment with an attempt at a witty retort. "I suppose guts on the table are bound to get eaten." When he didn't laugh she suddenly felt uncomfortable and moved over to the fireplace, deciding to change the subject. "I've always liked fires."

Dan lost his pensive look and stood next to her. "Warm fire, good music, bad-for-you food, what could be better?"

"Only thing that would make this perfect is Ryan and Kelly showing up. Of course, I'd have to turn off the music and apologize for the raunchy food," she said, smiling at him.

Dan winked and took out his cell to call Kelly. Although his phone showed one bar, he couldn't get any reception. Jenny's phone had been rendered useless the moment they drove into the mountains. He opened the door to hold his phone outside. Wind and snow whipped through the little cabin, nearly blowing out the fire. He quickly slammed the door shut. "Damn, it's turning into a full-blown blizzard. I'm afraid if they don't arrive soon, it'll be too late."

After another hour passed, Jenny began pacing. "I'm really worried about them."

"Jenny, neither Ryan nor Kelly would risk their lives if the roads are bad. They must be waiting out the storm. We'll see them tomorrow."

"Yeah, okay. You're right. Both are extremely practical." She took a deep breath to calm herself and then started checking through the closet for her favorite game to keep her mind occupied. "Hey, do you know what happened to Settlers of Catan? It was here the last time we came up."

He opened his mouth to reply when the lights suddenly went out. "Oh shit."

The lights sputtered on for a couple of seconds and then went dead again. The glow from the fire cast eerie shadows on Dan's face. "Did we just lose power?" she whimpered.

"Yep, we're screwed." He threw the last few logs on the fireplace. "I'll get more wood in the morning, but I think we'd better head to bed before all the heat is gone."

Jenny opened her bedroom door to allow the heat to enter. It was already freezing cold in the tiny room. The wind outside howled angrily and Jenny could feel a breeze coming from the window. She quickly donned her flannels in the dark and jumped into the bed. Jenny yelped when she slipped under the cold sheets.

"You okay in there?" Dan called out.

"Yeah, just a freezing bed. I'm fine." Jenny shivered until her body heat started to warm the covers. It seemed like hours before she fell asleep.

Her own teeth chattering woke her back up a short time later. She had never felt so cold in her life. Jenny wrapped the blankets tighter around herself, but it didn't help. She stared at the wooden slats above her. How did the pioneers do it? This was fucking nuts. She curled her toes under her and put her hands in her armpits. She tried to fall asleep, but woke up to her own moaning. It was just too damn cold!

She cried out when she saw movement in the doorway. "It's just me," Dan said. "I heard you whimpering."

Jenny's teeth chattered when she answered. "I'm so cold."

"Me, too. If you are not opposed, I think we should share our heat." She nodded vigorously, desperately needing his warmth. "My room feels a little warmer than yours," he offered.

Jenny pulled the blankets off the bed and followed him to the other bedroom. They piled all the covers onto his bed and she slipped under them. Jenny tried not to think how weird it was to be spooning Dan. He wrapped his arms around her and pressed up close. When she shifted to get more comfortable, she heard him catch his breath. Spooning Dan was definitely weird, but she was grateful for his body heat. Eventually his warmth radiated through her and her teeth stopped chattering.

"Better?" he asked.

"Much," Jenny said drowsily, falling asleep soon after. The blizzard continued to swirl around the little cabin, but she survived the night in relative comfort.

Dan was the first to stir the next morning. "I don't want to do this."

"Do what?" she asked groggily.

"Get out of this warm bed."

Jenny laughed. "I don't blame you."

"Yeah, but unless I get the firewood, we'll have to stay here all day."

"I'll cheer you on from the bed."

"That's big of you," he grumbled good-naturedly just before making the mad dash. Jenny heard him zip up his coat and stomp his boots several times. Then she heard the creak of the door and a loud, "Oh shit!"

"What? What's wrong?"

"This is bad."

Curiosity made her brave the cold. Jenny gasped

when she saw the doorway completely blocked by snow, from top to bottom. "What the heck?"

"Yeah, we're, like, literally snowed in."

"What are we going to do?" she asked, trying to keep calm as she shivered in the frigid air. The thought of being snowed in completely freaked her out. With no electricity and no way to leave, she wasn't sure how they would survive the cold.

He confirmed her fears when he said, "I have to get that firewood, Jenny. We're not going to survive without it." Dan grabbed a pot and scooped out a pan full of snow. She followed him as he walked to the bathroom and tossed it in the tub. Jenny quickly put on her coat, shoes, and gloves and grabbed another pot. The two began the arduous task of digging out. The positive in helping Dan was that Jenny got exceedingly warm working so hard.

Once they broke through the top layer of the snow, they were hit with blowing winds. The blizzard was still raging on. It took hours before they were able to dig their way to the woodpile. When Jenny hit the first log, she grabbed onto Dan, jumping up and down enthusiastically. "I found it! We're saved!"

He hugged her and laughed with relief. "I never thought we would see that damn wood." After digging out the woodpile, she helped him carry the logs into the cabin. The wood completely lined one wall. Lucky for them, there was a healthy supply. "I bet this will last at least a week," Dan assured her.

By the time they finished stacking the last of it,

both were starving. Jenny got out the donuts, precooked bacon and chocolate milk, grateful that they had chosen food that didn't need preparation. After he got a fire going, she took a cast-iron pot and filled it with snow. "Coffee soon," she announced, putting it on the edge of the fire.

"Great. By the way, thanks for all the help."

"Of course."

"Kelly would have sat on the sidelines and told me I was taking too long."

Jenny chuckled. "Yeah, she probably would have. Nice thing about working together is that we get to drink hot coffee sooner."

"Yep, can't wait." Dan put his hands next to the fire, rubbing them together vigorously.

As she stared into the flames, she started thinking about Ryan and fear gripped her heart. "You don't think they are stuck out there, do you?" Tears threatened to run down her cheeks when she thought of Ryan freezing in his car.

Dan walked over and put his arm around her. "No. I'm confident both are fine. Thankfully, we have enough supplies to wait out the storm. There's no need to worry, Jenny. Trust me."

She hesitantly pressed her head on his chest. For just a moment, she allowed herself to receive comfort in Dan's embrace. Then Jenny grabbed a hot pad and poured the boiling water into two cups, stirring in the instant coffee. "Here you go, made fresh by me."

"Nice." He cupped the mug in his hands.

"Nothing like a cup of hot coffee."

"Agreed." Jenny took a sip and cried out. "Hot! Too hot!"

Dan got up and opened the door. He came back with a handful of snow. He broke it in half, plopping one in her cup and handing her the other. "For your tongue."

Jenny took it gratefully, stuffing the icy snow into her burning mouth. "Aww... bewwer," she mumbled.

They spent the afternoon chatting about random stuff, trying to pass the time. After a few games of poker using pretzel sticks as money, Jenny started a more personal conversation. "So, when are you and Kelly planning on tying the knot?"

"Not sure it'll ever happen."

"Why not?" she asked, taken aback by his answer. She had naturally assumed the two of them would get married.

"I talked about marriage once but Kelly told me it wasn't her thing. She doesn't want to ruin what we have going. I've decided it's for the best."

"Oh! Well, I guess I can understand that. Her parents' divorce did a number on Kelly. I suppose it is not too surprising she's scared to give it a try."

"What about you guys?"

"Ryan wants to wait until he makes junior partner. You know him, gotta have all his ducks in a row before we can officially announce an engagement."

Dan nodded his head knowingly. "That sounds about right. He does like everything planned out."

"Yep, that's my Ryan!" Jenny got up and brought back a bottle of wine. "I think we deserve to drink after such hard work this morning."

"Sure, pour me a glass while I throw another log on the fire." When Dan came back, Jenny had taken over the couch. She lifted her legs to make room for him. When he sat down, she put her feet in his lap. "What's this, couch hog?" he asked with amusement.

"Just wanted to put my feet up. Got a problem with that?" She lifted her glass and took a sip of merlot.

"You sounded suspiciously like Kelly just now."

Jenny choked on her wine and sputtered. "After years of being friends, I guess she's bound to rub off on me."

Dan asked casually, "You ever wonder what would have happened if you and I had met when we were single?"

"Um... no." Jenny quickly took her feet off Dan's lap and sat up. "Why?"

"No reason."

"You aren't getting off that easy. You brought it up, so speak."

Dan gazed at her with his dark brown eyes shining in the firelight. "I don't know. We seem to click, don't you think? I've always thought we'd make a good couple."

"Where's this coming from, Dan? We're both taken."

"Yeah, I know. Still, I'm attracted to you."

"Are you making a pass at me?" she asked incredulously.

"No, just stating a fact. It's obvious the attraction is one-sided. Don't give it another thought."

The Seduction

After that revelation, what else *could* she think about? Jenny jumped off the couch and stood next to the fireplace. Her face was flushed and she didn't want Dan to see it. Of course she thought he was attractive. Who wouldn't? Kelly had great taste in men and Dan was her crowning glory.

At six feet five, Dan was a striking hunk of manhood. Although he didn't have a muscular frame, he was definitely fit. Jenny liked the adorable way his blond hair fell in his eyes when he got excited and the cute way he brushed it back with his fingers. Up to this point, she really hadn't thought about him romantically. Well, that wasn't quite true. She had fantasized about Dan a couple of times, but nothing serious. He was Kelly's guy.

"Didn't mean to make you uncomfortable," Dan said from the couch.

"That's okay. Like you said, we'll just forget it. So, how long do you think it will take before the bulldozers come to rescue us?"

"I don't know. All depends on if this blizzard was local or widespread."

"But you said we'll be okay."

"Yes, Jenny. Of that, I have no doubt."

She turned back to Dan. Even though her face was still flushed, he'd assume it was from the heat of the fire. "Okay, then I'll try not to worry... too much."

"Up for another game of poker? I'm ahead of you by five pretzels."

Her competitive streak took over and she joined him in a four-hour battle. Unfortunately, she was still behind at the end, but vowed total annihilation the next day. "I think I'll sleep out here tonight," she told Dan as they readied for bed.

"Okay. If you can, keep the logs on the fire so we don't freeze during the night."

"Not a problem." Jenny gathered her blankets off his bed and wrapped them around her as she lay on the couch. Things felt different now. After Dan's declaration, she needed to stay clear of him for her own good. Being close would only ignite something neither of them needed.

Naturally, Jenny slept so soundly that the fire went out. She woke to Dan starting it back up. She rolled off the couch wanting to help. "I'm sorry, Dan."

"No problem. Go back to bed. I was just freezing and figured you were asleep." He got a roaring fire going and headed back to his room.

She knew he was cold and took pity on him. "Wait."

Dan turned around. "Yeah?"

"Come over until your room gets warm." She sat up and lifted the blankets. Dan walked over and she threw the covers over him. They sat there in the dark watching the fire. Jenny was exceedingly aware of his body being so close to hers. Even though they weren't touching, she could feel the cold radiating off his skin. She moved over and pressed against him, giving him some of her warmth. It was the least she could do after letting the fire die.

"Thanks," he said, not moving a muscle.

The crackle of the fire was soothing. The way the light shifted and flickered over the walls had a hypnotic quality to it. "Dan?"

He turned his head towards her. Jenny felt the sudden urge to kiss him. She lifted her chin so that their lips met. An exhilarating thrill coursed through her body when he pressed his mouth against hers. She pulled away in shock, having never felt that before.

"Wow," he murmured. After a few seconds he asked, "Was it good for you?"

"Yeah, like scary good."

"Likewise."

They sat staring at the flames again. Jenny was unsure what to do. A kiss was excusable. Not good, but excusable. More than that and they were asking for trouble.

"I think my room is warm enough," Dan said,

getting up and moving away from her. She noticed he walked stiffly.

"I'll see you in the morning," Jenny called after him.

Dan waved his hand without looking back. He closed the door, shutting out any chance of warmth. Why would he do that?

She lay back down on the couch, trying to forget the way his kiss made her feel. The growing wetness between her legs belied her attempt. Maybe Dan was in that room jerking off while thinking of her. The thought turned her on. A short time later, he cracked the door open and went back to bed.

She was jealous of a man's ability to do that. Just a simple hand motion on their hard member and they could find release. Her? Masturbation never worked, but tonight she was desperate. Jenny fumbled with her clit, getting her fingers all wet in the process. She rubbed it this way and that, but all it ever produced was more tension, not blessed release. Finally, she gave up in frustration. She squeezed her legs tightly shut and forced herself to think about work. It was hours before she was able to fall back to sleep. It seemed like only moments later when she heard Dan moving logs onto the fire.

"Morning, sunshine."

"What? It's morning already?"

"Yep, got you a cup of joe on the counter there if you want it."

Jenny wiped the sleep from her eyes and assaulted with her musky smell. She put her hands down quickly, blushing. Jenny washed her hands in the melted snow in the kitchen sink. Then she grabbed the hot mug and drank its warm goodness. "Just the right temp," she purred.

"Good." Dan walked over to the counter and picked up his own mug, standing a little too close. "So how did you sleep?"

Jenny's heartbeat increased being in such close proximity, so she took a step back. There was no way she was about to tell him the truth. "Probably as well as you."

"Not well, huh?"

She crinkled her brow. "You didn't sleep?"

"Not really. Couldn't get you off my mind."

Jenny's pulse increased. Knowing he had spent the night thinking about her was hard to take. "You probably shouldn't tell me that."

"Why?"

"We are stuck here, Dan. We need to be adults about this."

"I was thinking about that, actually. You know as well as I do that both Ryan and Kelly are going to assume something happened no matter what we say. It's just the way things are. Two attractive people stuck in a cabin for a week…it's bound to happen."

"What's your point?"

"Well, if we are going to be accused of it anyway, why not enjoy the experience?"

Jenny shook her head. "You just won't give up, will you?"

"After last night's kiss? No way."

She blushed, thinking back on the experience. "It was a fluke. It's the whole stolen kiss thing. That's all it was."

"Wanna prove it?"

She scoffed at him. "Yeah, right."

"No, seriously. If we kiss and we don't both feel something, I'll stop hounding you. Cross my heart." Dan made a cross motion over his heart and smiled charmingly.

"You're pathetic, you know that?"

"I think you're chicken because you know I'm right."

"Don't start with me. You know I hate being called a chicken."

He nodded with a grin. "Yes, I do."

Jenny rolled her eyes and walked over to Dan. Here in the daylight with no romantic fire things would be different. He tried to put his arms around her, but she stopped him. "You said nothing about hugging, mister. A kiss. That's it."

A smile played across his lips. "Fine." Dan put his hands behind his back and waited.

She tried to calm the butterflies as she tiptoed up to kiss him. For a second she hesitated, afraid that he might be right—but no. She knew better and needed to prove it. Jenny gently pressed her mouth against his firm lips. He snuck a hand around and grasped the back of her neck. He slipped his tongue into her mouth and she felt fireworks go off. The desire she had felt all night instantly reignited. She unwillingly moaned and had to pull away. It was

19

disconcerting.

Dan's hair fell in his eyes and he brushed it back all cute-like. "Well?"

Jenny turned from him. "Didn't feel a thing."

He snuck up behind her and growled softly in her ear, "Yeah, I'm buying that."

Her heart raced when she felt the warmth of his breath on her neck. "Please don't."

"Don't what?" Dan asked, as he moved her hair aside and gently kissed the back of her neck.

She felt an electric jolt travel straight to her groin. "Don't make me want you."

Dan chuckled warmly. "But you already do."

Jenny closed her eyes. Her body was desperate for more, but they couldn't. It wasn't in the cards for them. She pulled away and pretended to straighten the kitchen.

Dan let out a frustrated sigh. "Okay, you win. I'll stop hounding you."

She felt almost disappointed. "Good, why don't we finish our poker game?"

"Fine," Dan grumbled. Then he added condescendingly, "I don't see the point. You are so behind now you don't have a chance of catching up."

"Oh yeah? We'll see about that." She dealt out the cards. In no time flat, she was out of pretzels. "How did you do that?"

"I'm on a winning streak and you're not."

Jenny pouted. She hated to lose and today it was especially humiliating. "I demand a rematch."

"Nope. You need collateral in order to play. I do

have a suggestion though. You could bet with clothing."

"Strip poker? You can't be serious."

"I am completely serious," Dan answered with a devilish glint in his eye. He started dealing out the cards. "You in?"

So much for him giving up on getting her in bed, but Jenny eagerly took up the challenge. "Okay, but only if I can pull out of the game at any time."

"It's a deal."

Jenny was pleasantly surprised when she beat his hand. "Since I'm the winner, I get to pick the piece of clothing," she announced.

"Okay by me."

"Your sweater."

Dan kept a straight face as he pulled it over his head. Jenny couldn't help gazing at his naked chest. She had only seen him shirtless from a distance once when she watched him play basketball outside Kelly's apartment. His defined chest with blond curls was quite distracting, and she had to look away.

"Your turn to deal."

Jenny looked down at the cards. Seeing his skin unnerved her. Jenny shuffled the cards and dealt them out. It seemed her luck had changed for good when she won the next hand too. "Your belt."

"Interesting choice," Dan replied, as he undid the buckle and whipped it out of the belt loops. The sound of the buckle hitting the floor made her blush. She was glad he couldn't tell what she was thinking.

Dan dealt the next hand. Jenny won with a pair of queens. She whistled enthusiastically. "I am on a roll now, baby! Socks next."

"Both?"

"Yep."

He dutifully took off his socks, exposing the manly fur on his feet. Dan wiggled his toes for her benefit. She quickly dealt out the next hand and then stopped. Was he losing on purpose? Jenny raised her eyebrow and stared at him.

"What?"

"My sudden winning streak seems a little suspicious."

"I see. You doubt your own card skills."

Jenny puckered her lips in concentration. She finished dealing and let out a happy squeal when she saw her hand, totally forgetting to keep a poker face. Jenny laid down two aces in triumph and then gasped when Dan showed her a three of a kind. He grinned mischievously. "Take off your top."

She shook her head. "I can't."

"Do not shirk on a bet, Jenny. It's bad manners."

In a quick move so she wouldn't second-guess herself, Jenny whipped off her sweater. She was grateful that her bra hid her assets. Jenny looked over at the fire, not wanting to see the expression on Dan's face.

"Nice. Not quite what I was expecting, but nice."

Jenny glanced down at her chest and burned with mortification. She had forgotten she was wearing her ancient smiley face bra. It was her most comfortable intimate apparel, but definitely not her sexiest. Ryan never cared what she wore.

"Enough gawking. Just deal the cards."

Dan chuckled and dealt the next hand. Jenny's heart raced. She had three Jacks and laid them down with a whoop. Dan smiled and showed her a flush. "Bra."

Jenny sputtered. "Not the bra. Let me take off my socks."

"Nope. The bra that keeps smiling back at me must go."

Jenny's hands trembled as she unclasped the back and slowly let her favorite bra fall from her shoulders. Dan's expression changed from amusement to adoration in the blink of an eye. Jenny blushed and instinctively covered her chest with her hands, suddenly feeling vulnerable.

"No, you have to let me see them. It's the rules."

Jenny's body tingled as she removed her hands and let him look at her breasts. "Had enough?" she finally asked.

"Never."

She picked up the deck and started shuffling. Dan's eyes never left her chest. Jenny quickly fanned her cards out and put them in front of her, effectively blocking his view.

Thankfully, she won with a king high. With

more enthusiasm than she meant to reveal, Jenny cried out, "Pants!"

Dan feigned shyness as he slowly stood up and undid the button on his jeans. He let them fall to the floor. Jenny couldn't help noticing the large bulge in his boxers. "Like what you see?"

The heat rushed to her cheeks. "Not really."

"That's only because you can't see what's underneath."

"I think I am done with the game."

"So soon? You were winning."

"Somehow, either way it seems *you* are the one winning."

He shrugged his shoulders. "If you want to wimp out, that's your business. But the rules state that we both have to keep our clothes off for the rest of the day."

Jenny had a sneaking suspicion he was making it up, but she was willing to play along. "Better put some more logs on the fire then, I feel a little cold."

"I can tell," he said with a smirk, gazing brazenly at her nipples.

"Me, too." She smiled wickedly, staring at his crotch. Dan moved to put more wood on, laughing under his breath.

Jenny found herself admiring his ass as he bent over to stoke the fire. She shook her head. What the hell was she doing? "We can't have sex, Dan," she blurted. "I would never forgive myself."

Once Dan had a hot fire going, he turned around and asked, "What constitutes overstepping the bounds? How far is too far?"

Jenny frowned. She hadn't thought about it before. "Well, we definitely can't make love. My vagina is off limits."

"Okay."

"So what does that really leave? I don't think it's worth even bothering with."

"I disagree. It leaves us many options I'm open to exploring. What about you?"

Ryan and she pretty much just fucked. Every now and then, they did a little oral but neither of them was much into it. Jenny felt rather sorry for Dan. Without penetration, neither would have much fun. "Well, I suppose if you're still willing I am."

"Good." Dan walked over and pulled her close, kissing Jenny without even asking. Her breasts pressed against his naked chest. The electricity it caused left Jenny breathless afterwards. It might be a little enjoyable after all. "What do you want to try first?" he asked.

Jenny sighed. "What? You want me to suck on you?" It seemed the most obvious choice.

"Nah, how about you play with yourself while I watch."

Jenny looked at him in horror. "No way. I can't do that."

"Why not? I've fantasized about it for years."

She hated to admit the truth, but figured honesty was the best policy. "I don't do that really. I guess I'm one of those weird girls who only like cock."

"I don't buy it."

"Well, it's a fact. Want me to suck on you now?"

"No. I want to help you play with yourself."

Jenny felt her whole body flush. "I can't do that, Dan. It'd be too embarrassing."

"Why?" He leaned over and whispered hoarsely, "Nothing would turn me on more than watching you get yourself off."

Even though Jenny knew she was facing certain humiliation, she let Dan guide her to the couch. He slowly unbuttoned her jeans and pulled them down. She was grateful she'd worn lacy panties at least. Dan pulled off his boxers and lay on the sofa, motioning her to join him. Jenny stared at his thick cock. It was definitely different from Ryan's long, thin one.

Jenny hesitantly lay down next to him, staring up at the log ceiling, afraid to make eye contact. Dan took her hand and moved it to her pussy. "Play with yourself." Jenny reluctantly stuck her hand under her panties and fumbled with her clit like she always did. "That's sweet," he murmured. He shimmied off her underwear and put his finger next to hers. Dan started rubbing at a faster rate, applying more pressure than she ever did. It instantly caused a warm sensation throughout her groin area. "Now you try it," he told her.

Jenny had to swallow her pride as she attempted to flick herself with the same enthusiasm he had. "Faster," he encouraged. Soon her sensitive clit was singing under her own touch. She felt his hard cock push into her thigh, the wetness of his precome leaving a trail on her leg. There was no doubt that Dan enjoyed watching her.

"I am *not* going to enter you with my fingers, have no fear. I just want to touch your luscious pussy while you play with yourself."

Jenny stifled a gasp when he felt around her inner lips. It was thrilling to have his fingers exploring her while she stimulated her clit.

"So wet and swollen. I can tell you're close, Jenny." His confidence and manly touch heightened her arousal. The fact that Dan was about to witness her first manual orgasm excited her for some reason. He leaned down and sucked on her breast for the first time. She cried out and felt a strong contraction in her loins. "So close..." he whispered and then sucked her nipple harder.

Jenny closed her eyes as the fire between her legs reached a level she'd never gotten to before. Her back automatically arched as another contraction hit sending her over the edge. Jenny whimpered in pleasure as wave after wave rolled over her.

"So damn sexy," Dan growled after her climax ended. He took her wet hand and placed it on his cock. Jenny shifted so she was facing him and then she started stroking his shaft. "Kiss me. This won't take long."

Dan plundered her lips while Jenny caressed his thick tool vigorously. He groaned in her mouth as he stiffened. Jenny felt his cock spasm just before hot come shot onto her stomach. His dick continued pulsating in her hand as he released a full load.

He opened his eyes and smiled at her. "I told you it wouldn't take long."

"Is that normally the case for you?" she asked innocently, although it was meant as a joke.

He gazed at her with tender emotion. "No, only when I'm in the presence of a woman I've wanted for far too long."

Jenny had no witty retort to fire back. "Ah…"

Dan kissed her cheek. "Did you enjoy it?"

"More than I thought," she admitted.

"Good, because this is only the beginning."

Jenny laughed as she scooted off the couch and got up. "This was a one-time deal, Dan."

"Oh no, we have days together and I plan to take full advantage of them."

"In your dreams."

After they cleaned up, Dan suggested the two of them get dressed since the night air was creeping into the cabin. They spent the evening sipping wine and talking about their childhoods. Dan asked Jenny to put her feet on his lap while they talked. He massaged them in the most delightful way while they shared more about themselves.

"I've always felt jealous of Kelly when you rubbed her feet," Jenny confessed. "Ryan can't stand feet. He almost gagged the one time he rubbed them for me."

"Ryan is a fool. These are beautiful feet."

Jenny felt bad for complaining, so she hastily added, "Hey, don't get me wrong. Ryan is amazing in bed. We can go for hours."

"I'm sure," answered Dan, bending over and kissing each toe. The intimate gesture made her tremble inside. Man, he was a good lover.

Snowy Interlude

It was a relief to Jenny when he went to sleep in his own room. She was afraid that with too much contact, she'd forget her vow not to make love to him. Jenny held onto the notion that a little fingering wasn't dangerous. In fact, she had learned something valuable.

Jenny snuck her fingers underneath her panties and began playing with herself. Her body was still on fire and quickly responded to her touch. She kneaded and pulled on her nipple as she vigorously flicked her clit. She made herself incredibly wet in the process, but she needed something more. Jenny stuck her finger inside her eager pussy, trying not to think of Dan. Jenny cried out softly when her orgasm finally hit. *Success!*

She snuggled down in the covers afterwards and purred. Having the power to make herself come was incredible. Jenny fell asleep with a huge smile on her lips.

In the middle of the night, she was surprised to wake up from an erotic dream to see Dan standing over her with an obvious hard-on. "What?" she asked in astonishment, quickly sitting up and moving to the other side of the couch.

"What you do mean what? You were calling my name."

She smirked as it had been a *really* good dream. "You must have been hearing things. I was asleep."

"No, I heard you clearly. You were moaning, 'Oh Dan, yes…yes! I want it harder, Dan!'"

Jenny blushed, recalling how hard he had pounded her in the dream. "I think you are making that up," she insisted.

"Well, maybe the 'I want it harder' part. But you were definitely calling my name, so here I am."

Jenny looked at his masculine cock standing so proud and erect. "I'm not sure how you can help me."

"Well, then maybe you can help me. Have you ever had someone make love to your breasts?"

"Can't say that I have."

"Mind if I fulfill that little fantasy? You have gorgeous breasts, Jenny."

The passion in her dream clearly influenced her answer. "I suppose you can make love to my breasts, Dan. Just be gentle."

"Let me add a few more logs to the fire and get the lubricant."

It involved lube? Jenny wondered what she was in for. When he returned she asked, "What are you doing with a tube of lubricant anyway? Seems a little odd."

"Kelly and I are fairly adventurous. I always bring it with me in case we decide to enjoy a little extracurricular fun."

Once again, Jenny felt jealous of Kelly. Ryan certainly could fuck for hours, but there wasn't any real variety to it.

"Take off your top," Dan instructed as he knelt down beside her. He squeezed the gel in his hand and gently rubbed it on her chest. Her nipples were already hard even before the lubricant made contact, but the coldness made her jump. "Sorry about that." He kissed each nipple tenderly before straddling her on the couch. Dan placed his hard cock in between her full breasts. "Push them together for me," he asked.

Jenny took each hand on either side of her breasts and pressed them against his shaft. Dan put his hands on hers and pushed them even more, so that her flesh enveloped his entire dick. "Keep it like that."

Dan started stroking his shaft in and out of her cleavage. She watched as the head of his cock popped out and then disappeared back into her firm mountains of sexy flesh. It was visually exciting, especially when she looked up and saw the look of ecstasy on Dan's face.

He started thrusting his hips with more force, as if he was taking her pussy. Jenny saw his cock leaking come and knew he was thoroughly enjoying the friction of her breasts. She closed her eyes, imagining his dick inside her thrusting hard and taking her deep. She unconsciously lifted her hips in rhythm with his strokes.

When he started grunting, she opened her eyes. Jenny watched with interest as Dan came. He threw his head back and started groaning. She felt her juices flow when he cried out in pleasure. Jenny opened her lips and let his come shoot onto her tongue. It was incredibly tangy to the point of almost being bitter. Dan slowly eased his dick further into her mouth and finished coming inside her. "Incredible," he breathed, shuddering after his climax.

Dan looked down at her with a look she couldn't place. "I am a very happy man." He flipped his hair back before lifting himself off and moving down between her legs. "Now to make you a happy woman. I desperately want my fingers inside your pussy so I can stroke your G-spot, but I won't. I hope your come will still be just as sweet."

Jenny wasn't expecting much when Dan first licked her clit. Ryan had performed cunnilingus before and she found it rather boring. She turned her head towards the fire and watched the flames dance on the wood. She was surprised when she felt him sucking on her clit. All Ryan ever did was lick it a few times. The more Dan sucked, the hotter her pussy became.

Then Jenny felt his fingers exploring her swollen lips. His light touch teased her hole, coming close but never penetrating her eager depths. She jumped a little when his index finger pressed against her anus; no one had ever touched her there before. Jenny shifted, but Dan moved with her, his finger firmly in place. "Don't fight it, Jenny. Let me touch you. I promise you will like it," he murmured.

He continued his sucking assault on her sensitive nodule as he slowly pushed the tip of his finger into her ass. Jenny squirmed, but he said softly, "Don't move. Let your body get used to it."

She lay still, her heart palpitating as his finger slowly penetrated her. There was something so primal about the invasion. Jenny was surprised it was making her even wetter.

"Good girl," he murmured in a low voice. He started flicking his tongue over her clit, matching the rhythm as he slowly thrust his finger in and out of her anus. What had always been a boring part of foreplay had suddenly become hot and nasty.

Dan continued to stroke her ass with his finger as his tongue danced over her clit. The pressure slowly built until she felt ready to explode. Jenny pressed her clit against his mouth. He started suckling it, sending the heat throughout her entire body. This time a cold chill took over before she felt the first wave of her orgasm. Her pussy convulsed repeatedly as she came on Dan's mouth. He pulled out his finger just before the final contraction ended.

Her thighs were trembling when she lifted her head to thank him. "That was better than I expected."

Dan looked up between her legs. "I thought you'd like that."

Instead of going back to his room, Dan stayed with Jenny on the couch. They curled up together with his arm draped over her. Jenny fell asleep immediately in his embrace.

The next morning she woke up to Dan's breath on her neck. It gave her tingling chills. Why didn't she feel that way with Ryan? He was a good guy and she'd never had complaints before. But damn, he *never* made her feel like this.

When Dan finally stirred, she got off the couch and gathered breakfast materials. Dan automatically went to stoke the fire. They sat at the table staring at each other in silence while they ate a cold breakfast and drank their instant coffee.

Dan finally asked, "Have you ever deepthroated a guy?"

Jenny looked at him in shock. "Are you kidding? I don't like to gag when I suck a man."

"Oh, okay."

She had expected he would argue the point, but he didn't. He continued eating his cinnamon Pop-Tart and sipping his coffee in silence.

"Does Kelly deepthroat you?"

"Nah. She's like you."

Dan got up and threw another log on the fire before getting a pan of snow to melt for water. He announced from the door, "It looks like things are finally clearing up. The wind has died down and the sun's out today."

"Good," Jenny said, but she was secretly disappointed.

In the afternoon, after a card game of Liar, which she dominated, Jenny brought up the subject of deepthroating again. His suggestion had frightened her when he first mentioned it, but the more she thought about the act the more curious she was to try it. "So, I don't even know how to deepthroat a guy."

"Would you like to learn?"

Jenny didn't answer immediately. She shuffled the cards a couple of times and then put the stack down on the table and looked at him. "Maybe."

"If you want to practice with me, I'd be happy to show you the ropes."

"How many girls have taken you that way?"

"Only one, but it's an experience I've never forgotten."

She was honest with him. "I'm afraid I'll choke."

"I would take it slow with you. Just fun and practice. No pressure at all."

Jenny sighed nervously. Why did she have such a burning desire to please him? It wasn't natural. "Okay, how do we start?"

Dan cleared off the kitchen table. "This seems to be the perfect height. I noticed it this morning." He motioned her to him. Jenny was about to get on the table, but Dan grabbed her in his arms. He kissed her neck and then lightly nibbled on her collarbone. "You are one sexy woman, Jenny." Dan poured wine for both of them and handed her a glass. It was still a little early for drinking, but Jenny took it realizing it would help her relax.

Dan relieved Jenny of her shirt and bra. He was so natural about it that she found herself half-naked before she knew what was happening. He leisurely caressed her breasts and then started kissing her on the lips. Dan teased her mouth with that naughty tongue of his. Oh, his kisses were trouble. She'd do anything for him now.

Once her body was properly tingling in anticipation, Dan asked her to lie down on the table. He helped her lie face up and then pulled her towards him until her head hung slightly off the edge. "The right angle is everything," he told her, running his hand over her throat with a lustful look in his eye.

She was trying to act calmer than she felt, but she couldn't control how quickly her breasts were rising and falling and he noticed. Dan knelt down beside her and said, "Don't be scared. We'll end it if it's something you don't like."

Jenny's entire body relaxed. There was no reason to be scared. She trusted Dan and this was something she wanted to try. Jenny watched him with her upside-down view as he took off his clothes in front of her. Dan's cock looked eager for the practice session.

"There are a few things that will make this easier. First, we need you to get a lot of saliva going. The more the better. Don't worry about slurping sounds or it dripping from your mouth. It's a good thing. Second, you are going to control my cock and the depth of it at all times. I will not thrust into you. Thirdly, breathe in when you push in and exhale when you push out. The most important thing of all is when you hit the back of your throat and you don't think you can take anymore, that's when you need to swallow. If you swallow my cock into your throat you won't feel the need to gag."

Jenny opened her mouth to let him know she was ready. When Dan moved closer, she took his cock in her hand. In order to build up saliva, Jenny sucked and nibbled on the head of his shaft first. Then she started taking him into her mouth—not all at once, but little by little. She teased him mercilessly because she had all the control. Dan groaned time and time again as she brought him to the edge, making him plead for her to stop.

There came a point when she knew she was ready. Jenny held him tighter and pulled his shaft into her, letting it travel further than she had before. When it reached the back of her throat, she forgot to swallow and gagged instead. He instantly pulled out. "That was good for your first try," he complimented.

"I want to try again."

"Are you sure?"

She took his shaft and guided it into her wide-open lips. When she got to that point again, she forced herself to swallow. His cock moved in further, blocking her breathing. It frightened her, even though she'd been warned. Jenny pulled him back out. Dan smiled down at her, ready to end their first session but Jenny wasn't done trying.

She guided his cock back to her. Dan had a look of surprise as he watched his dick disappear into her mouth again. Now that Jenny's body knew what to expect, she was sure she could do it. She took a breath in and swallowed, feeling his cock start down her throat. She pushed him a little deeper and Dan groaned in ecstasy. The tightness in her throat resisted his girth. That was all she could manage and she pulled him out for the last time.

"Amazing, you did amazing." He bent over and kissed her. Dan brushed a wet lock of hair from her cheek. "I can't believe how incredible you are, Jenny." He gently pushed her back on the table so her head wasn't hanging over and then he walked to the door. Dan opened it and grabbed a handful of snow. He came back with a mischievous smile. "Have you ever…"

"The answer is no, Dan. Just assume that."

Dan chuckled and pulled off her remaining clothes. He stared at Jenny for a while, seeming to drink in the vision of her. "I'm going to make love to you with snow. I hope you like it cold."

"Not sure that I do, but I am willing to find out."

He took the snow and rubbed it against her right nipple. It instantly hardened as the ice crystals melted on her warm skin.

"Oh," she yelped.

Dan smiled as he slid the melting snow onto her

other nipple. His warm lips came down on the first one. Jenny moaned in pleasure, the temperature contrast a pure delight. "I take it you like snow."

"I do now," she purred.

Dan rubbed it over her stomach, making her jump and squirm. His warm tongue followed the watery trail he made. She groaned when he teasingly brought it close to her mound, but soon all the snow had melted. Dan grabbed a pot and went outside to get some more. Jenny lay there on the table quivering in anticipation. She laughed when she saw the heaping amount he brought back. "You better not use all that on me."

"I didn't want to chance leaving you again," he answered. Dan shaped a handful of snow into a small ball and moved down to her leg. Starting at the arch of her foot, he slid the freezing ball slowly up her leg past her knee. Jenny wiggled the closer he got. The snow glided across the crease of her butt cheek, the drips tickling as they fell. The icy ball finally made its way up to her mound. She squealed when it touched her clit, but then he took it away. Just like last time, Dan followed the wet trail with his tongue, starting at her foot and ending up on her clit.

Dan made another ball. Jenny smiled and closed her eyes when he started on her left leg. All of her senses were focused on his frozen caress and scorching tongue. She had never thought of snow as a sexual tool before. Jenny couldn't help it, she squealed again when the snow glided onto her clit.

She was so hot down there that the temperature difference was shocking—in a good way.

Jenny wondered about his next move and was surprised to see Dan carefully shaping the snow into a phallus. Her eyes widened as he approached her with it. "What do you think you're doing?"

"No worries. I'm just going to slide it over your hot pussy. Lie back and trust me."

She did as he asked, her nipples growing hard in anticipation. The thought of the frozen phallus touching her most intimate spot made her crazy. Jenny gasped when Dan slid it against her inner thigh, letting her feel its icy hardness. He ran it up and over her mound to the other side. The head of it slowly glided down her outer lips down to the valley near her anus. He slowly brought it back up between her juicy lips, water pouring from it as it contacted her burning sex. He hesitated at her opening but moved upward pressing the length of the shaft against her as the tip played with her quivering clit. A shudder went through her. He began rubbing the icy phallus against her, as if it were a real cock. She moved with it, liking the sensation it created.

The combination of ice and friction was delightfully maddening. Jenny had only one consuming desire. "Please, stick it in me," she whispered.

Dan moved the head of it back down to her opening. She held her breath as he slowly, painstakingly inserted the frosty shaft into her hot depths. Jenny whimpered and then cried out as the cold took over. Then Dan's warm lips encased her freezing clit, sucking… flicking… the intermingling of his hot mouth with the cold phallus melting inside her… it all was taking her to a higher state of intensity. "I'm coming," she suddenly moaned. Jenny grasped the edge of the table as her hips bucked against Dan's mouth in a powerful orgasm. She gasped as it rocked her and then she collapsed back on the table trembling. "Oh Dan, that was amazing," she breathed, rubbing his blond hair appreciatively.

He kissed her clit one last time and then crawled up between her legs to kiss her lips. He smelled and tasted of her. Jenny felt his hard, hot, throbbing cock on her stomach. "Don't move," he said. Dan started rubbing his shaft against her in small gentle movements. He kissed her again, darting his tongue inside her mouth. Jenny ran her hands down his buttocks, holding onto him as his manhood pulsated between them. It felt so intimate and sexy.

He continued pressing against her tummy, moving slowly and sensually while they French-kissed. He made guttural sounds as he climaxed on her. She felt the warmth of his ejaculation and moaned in response. Everything about the man was sexy.

Dan gazed down at her afterwards with an expression that looked suspiciously like love. Thankfully, instead of a declaration of affection, he said hoarsely, "Incredible."

Jenny smiled and lifted herself up, feeling a cascade of water pour out between her legs. "Poor snowy cock. It is no more."

Dan got a towel and sopped up the puddle after cleaning her off. "It never had a chance; your pussy was way too hot for it to survive. But what a way to go."

She giggled as he helped her off the table. Jenny felt her knees give and had to hold onto the edge for balance. "You make me weak."

Dan took pity on her and picked Jenny up, carrying her to the couch. "Rest, my little kumquat. Let your man provide you with sustenance."

She watched him gather a collection of their favorite foods and arrange them on a tray. It seemed so normal, like they had been a couple for years. The fact he said *your man* did not go unnoticed by her. It seemed Dan had feelings that ran far deeper than simple attraction. It frightened Jenny.

They both had partners who would be devastated if they became a couple. Should she say something to Dan now or just let it slide? Part of her wanted to keep the fantasy going, to pretend just a little longer. He brought the tray over and placed it on the coffee table with flourish. "Only the best for you, milady."

Jenny grabbed a cracker and put cheese and a slice of salami on it. She stuffed it in her mouth with relish. "Yum," she complimented with a full mouth, as he walked back to the kitchen.

Dan returned with hot chocolate. "After such a chilly interlude, I figured a little hot cocoa was in order."

"You think of everything." Jenny wrapped her fingers around the warm mug gratefully.

They spent the evening playing the board game Catan. Dan had recovered it out of an old trunk in his bedroom. Jenny was thrilled because it was her personal favorite. Dan proved to be a worthy opponent. The game lasted hours as the two worked against each other, both determined to win. Dan finally had to concede defeat, but wasn't satisfied until she agreed to a rematch. Jenny started setting up the board while he got up to stretch his legs and check the weather.

Dan opened the door and peeked outside. "Jenny, you need to see this!"

She finished setting up the board and joined him. The night sky was crystal clear and filled with millions of twinkling stars. More stars than Jenny had ever seen before. She could even make out the Milky Way. "Incredible…"

Dan put his arms around her as they gazed up at the sky together. "The universe is breathtaking in its splendor and size."

She pressed herself against his warm chest. "It's truly beautiful."

He bent down and blew hot air on her ear, sending a shiver through her soul. "Jenny."

"Yes?"

"There is something I'm desperate to do with you."

She giggled softly. "Oh yeah?" What else could he possibly have in mind?

His warm lips tickled her ear. "I want to come inside you."

Her groin ached pleasantly at the thought, but it wasn't a possibility. "We can't, you know that."

"We can. There is a way without compromising anything."

Jenny smiled, not believing him. "How?"

"Let me take you anally."

She couldn't breathe. The thought of taking his thick cock into her ass sounded painful. There was nothing sexy about it. "No. I don't want to."

He kissed her neck again. Dan walked back into the cabin and sat down beside the game board. She could tell he was disappointed. As much as she wanted to please him, Jenny couldn't go that far.

She looked back up at the stars with a sense of regret before shutting the door.

A Wicked Proposal

They played a second round of Catan, but neither was into it. Things were too quiet. In an attempt to lighten the mood, Jenny made martinis.

"You *do* make a damn good martini," Dan said, taking a sip of her concoction.

"Thank you, thank you," Jenny answered with a small curtsy.

The drink went straight to her head. While playing the game she concentrated on building a long and winding road instead of trying to beat Dan. He saw what she was doing and gradually created a smiley face with his road pieces. It took a while for Jenny to notice. Once she did, she started laughing and slapped him hard on the back.

Dan chuckled. "I concede, you win for longest road."

"Oh no, you win for creativity. In fact, you are the most creative guy I know." She gave him a quick peck on the cheek. "I've never had snow used on me before."

"You bring it out in me, Jenny. I want to love you in so many different ways."

He was getting far too serious. "Kelly is a lucky girl, Dan. I hope she knows that."

Dan looked at her with a pained expression. He said nothing, but got up and walked to his bedroom, shutting the door quietly behind him. Jenny sat alone on the couch feeling sad.

She slowly picked up the game pieces and added a log to the fire before curling up on the couch to stare at it. Jenny watched with interest as it licked the edges of the log. The wood seemed impervious to the hot flames, but they were relentless. Eventually the log caught fire and began to burn bright. She looked at Dan's door, then she got up and made herself another martini.

She sat next to the fireplace while sipping her drink. She wanted Dan; she couldn't deny that. Even if it cost her everything, Jenny needed to be in his arms tonight. When she finished her martini, she got up and walked to his door.

Jenny knocked lightly on the wooden frame. "Dan?"

After a minute, he opened it. Dan stood before her in nothing but his boxers. "Jenny."

She put her hands on his hairy chest and looked up into his dark brown eyes. "I... I'm willing to try."

Dan smiled as he took her hand and led her to

the bed. She lay down, feeling both nervous and exhilarated. He joined her and started running his hands over her skin. "Tonight your body will know what it means to be loved." He slowly took off each piece of clothing, lightly kissing the exposed flesh.

When he had her completely naked, she turned the tables and undressed him. Jenny pulled off his boxers and then tenderly kissed the head of his rigid cock. It was exciting to think that it would be deep inside her soon.

"Lie down on your back," he told her. Jenny was grateful that he wanted a little foreplay first. Dan began by massaging her feet. He took his time, lovingly caressing every part of her body, pulling the tension out and replacing it with anticipation. Dan spent more than an hour loving her body with his hands. Jenny had never felt so pampered or relaxed.

Then he leaned over her and pressed his lips against hers. She knew it was time. Dan fumbled through the drawer on the side table. He placed a dollop of gel in her hand and then directed it to his hard penis. Jenny rubbed it over his shaft, making sure every inch of it was covered in the slippery lubricant.

When she finished, he asked her to roll over on-to her stomach and spread her legs. Jenny felt the cold gel slide down between her buttocks. Dan massaged her anus and then gently pushed his finger inside to spread the lubricant further. He fingered her ass for several minutes, helping her taut muscles to relax. When he felt she was ready, he said, "Get on your hands and knees, Jenny. I want to make love to you."

Jenny's breath increased as she presented herself to him. She felt the bed shift and he moved up to her, placing his hands on her hips. "There's no rushing this. I am going to be gentle with you."

She looked back at him, struck by how handsome Dan looked getting ready to mount her. Jenny groaned in anticipation, her body hungering for him. She *needed* to meld with Dan.

He placed his cock against her puckered hole. She held her breath as Dan began pressing against it. "You have to breathe, Jenny."

She laughed nervously. "Guess I'm a little scared."

"Don't be. Rock back on my dick, I will follow your lead."

Jenny pushed against his large head, unsure how her body was ever going to take all of him. Dan's fingers moved down to her clit and he began stroking her as she rocked against his hard cock. The hotter her clit became, the more she needed to feel his shaft inside her. She started pushing with more determination and felt her muscles start to give. Suddenly, the entire head slipped in. She stopped, startled by the feeling of fullness.

"Give your body time," he murmured, running his hands over her back.

It hadn't hurt like she expected and the excitement of knowing Dan was inside her spurred her on. Jenny began rocking against his shaft, wanting to feel more of him. He placed both hands on her waist and moved in unison with her as if they'd been lovers for years. Each gentle thrust drove him deeper inside her. Jenny started moaning, taking pleasure in the fullness and resistance. It reminded her of having sex for the first time when everything was new and exhilarating.

Dan made a low guttural sound as his cock pushed fully into her depths. His pleasure thrilled her. She almost made the mistake of crying out, "I love you," and had to bite her tongue.

"You're so tight, Jenny. It's unreal."

She purred, "You feel good inside me, so good…"

He stopped for a moment. "Kiss me." She turned her head and they kissed with his cock pushed deep inside her. Her juices flowed as her body responded to the intimacy of it. Dan put his hands on her hips and slowly pushed in and out of her. It definitely felt different from vaginal penetration, but she liked the sensation and the feeling of being totally possessed by him. In this moment, she was *his*.

Dan's thrusts became longer and faster as her body conformed to his cock. "Yes, Dan, take me. Take all of me," she moaned.

He growled under his breath, "I don't want to come yet. I want this to last." Dan slowed down and reached between her legs, playing with her clit again. Jenny surprised herself by joining her fingers with his. Together they teased her clit. She couldn't believe how much Dan had changed her in such a short amount of time. She felt like a different woman now.

Jenny started moaning when the familiar heat began to build in her core. It must have been too much for Dan, because he stopped what he was doing and went back to stroking her with his cock, his thrusts fast and deep. "Jenny, I can't hold on any longer. I'm about to lose it."

"Come inside me, Dan. I *need* you to," she moaned.

His cock seemed to expand just before Dan cried out and his hot come erupted inside her. With all the extra nerve endings inside her ass, she could actually feel the warmth of his ejaculation. She loved the feeling of connection as he came.

After the last shudder of his orgasm, he lowered them both on the bed, turning her to the side with his cock still wedged inside her. He took his fingers and expertly teased her receptive button. In no time, she was squirming. "I want you to come for me," he growled in her ear.

She wanted to; she was desperate for it. "Yes, keep touching me just like that," she whimpered. Jenny felt the building contractions, each one more powerful than the next until she couldn't stand it any longer. The rhythmic heat between her legs transformed into waves of intense pleasure. Her back arched as she came, pushing herself against his body. When the last wave receded, Dan whispered, "I love you, Jenny."

She remained silent, wanting to answer him but knowing she couldn't. They were both taken. Ryan and Kelly deserved better than this. Their newfound love would ruin everything. Jenny closed her eyes. It was then that she realized what a fool she'd been. Having anal sex was just as intimate as vaginal sex. She had cheated on Ryan. There was no way around it.

She probably should have pulled away from Dan and gone to her own room, but she didn't. It felt too good lying there in his arms. Jenny felt tears forming. How she wished they had met when they were single. He was perfect for her. Not only as a lover, but also as a friend. The thought of being loved like this every day made her want to weep with joy. But this wasn't meant to be. They *hadn't* met when they were unattached and their futures were set. All Jenny had was this small moment in time to love him.

She heard his soft breathing and realized Dan was asleep. His warm breath sent chills every time he breathed out. She stared into the darkness. Tomorrow she would tell Dan she wanted to make love to him—to make love properly. Even though this love affair had no chance of a future, she could hold onto the memories. It would have to be enough.

Jenny couldn't wait to tell him in the morning. Dan would finally know that she returned his feelings. She was able to fall asleep soon after, excited about what tomorrow would bring.

Dan shook her on the shoulder and yelled, "Wake up!" She struggled to push out of her dream, but it was so nice she wanted to stay there. "Jenny, they're coming!"

Her eyes popped open. She looked at Dan in confusion. "What are you talking about?"

"Listen," he said earnestly.

She strained to listen and then she heard it, the far-off sound of an engine. *Not yet.* She glanced at Dan with a look of dread, not excitement.

"We have to get this cabin in order, make sure everything is in its proper place," Dan told her, throwing on his jeans and looking around for his shirt.

Jenny quickly dressed and joined him in picking up the cabin. Neither spoke as they cleaned up the place, hiding any evidence of their affair. Jenny searched his room and found a pair of her panties under the bed. She scooped them up and ran to her room, throwing them in her suitcase. She grabbed the blankets off the couch and quickly made her bed.

She came out of her bedroom and saw that Dan was adding more logs to the fire. Jenny decided to lay out breakfast foods so it would look like they were in the middle of eating. He set the pot on the fire for coffee and then turned towards her. Dan looked at Jenny longingly, in as much shock as she was. Their time was over...

The bulldozer was getting close, the engine noise echoing through the small mountain valley.

Jenny looked at Dan sadly. She wouldn't get the chance to show him how she felt. He would never know that she felt the same way. *Maybe it's for the best.*

Jenny thought of Ryan. A good man with a serious drive to succeed. A man she once saw herself spending the rest of her life with. He was her college sweetheart. Suddenly, she wondered if she loved him enough. She was afraid she would forever compare the two and she already knew Ryan would come up short.

But then there was Kelly, her best friend for over three years. The two of them were inseparable, like long-lost sisters. Kelly didn't deserve to be hurt. She could never know the terrible thing Jenny had done. If she ever learned of it, Jenny would lose Kelly forever.

Dan stared at her without saying a word. Life was about to return to 'normal' and Jenny wasn't ready for it. She walked over to him. "Dan, there is something you need to know before they get here."

"What? You want to pretend this never happened? I'm not sure I can, but if it's what you want I'll try."

"No, Dan. The fact is…"

The roaring engine of the bulldozer sounded like it was right outside the door. Time was running out. Jenny told him, "I love you."

Dan shook his head. It was obvious he hadn't heard her over the noise. She yelled it again just as the engine of the bulldozer cut out. The words "I love you!" rang through the cabin loud and clear.

He looked stunned. From outside, Jenny heard the slam of a car door and then Ryan called out, "Hey, is anyone home?"

"You're serious, Jenny?" Dan asked, looking as if he couldn't quite believe her.

Jenny heard the worry in Kelly's voice when she shouted from outside, "Are you guys okay in there?"

Dan grasped the back of her neck and kissed her passionately. Jenny returned his kiss, not wanting to let go. Finally, he broke the embrace just as Ryan and Kelly passed by the cabin window. "We have to tell them."

She nodded her head as she watched the doorknob slowly turn. With tears in her eyes Jenny replied, "I know…"

Blissfully in Love

Jenny trembled as the cabin door opened. She instinctively clutched Dan's sweaty hand and held on for dear life. This was it—they were about to ruin both their partners' lives. The intense love she felt for Dan after being snowbound together was undeniable. She was convinced it was worth this awful moment.

Ryan entered first, concern clearly written on his face when he laid eyes on Jenny. "I've been so worried about you! Are you okay, Jen?" He rushed to her, ignoring the fact she was clasping Dan's hand. When Ryan pulled her into his arms, she felt Dan let go...

Kelly, Jenny's best friend, was right behind Ryan. "I haven't been able to stop worrying. I had terrible dreams about you two up here." She threw her arms around Dan and sobbed.

Jenny couldn't help noticing that the two looked like the perfect pair, with their matching blond hair and sun-kissed skin.

Dan glanced at Jenny, his dark brown eyes communicating something she couldn't discern. Did he still want to tell them? Was he tempted to change his mind after seeing Kelly again?

Jenny was suddenly plagued with second thoughts about exposing the truth of their affair. She became even more uncertain when Dan hesitantly put an arm around her best friend and said, "We're fine."

Kelly buried her face in his chest. "I'm so relieved!"

Her quiet sobbing consumed Jenny with guilt. How could she have done this to Kelly? There was no way her best friend could ever forgive her for this.

Ryan finally released Jenny from his constricting but loving embrace. "We've been trying to reach you guys since Friday. It's been hell waiting out the storm." He brushed Jenny's midnight hair away from her face. "All I could think of was you freezing up here in the cabin, but I should have known better with that Cherokee blood running in your veins. You're a survivor through and through." Ryan kissed her on the lips, but Jenny couldn't return the kiss. He cocked his head, his emerald eyes filled with renewed concern. "What's wrong, Jen?"

She looked back over at Dan, unsure if she should say something.

Dan cleared his throat. "Kelly. Ryan. There is something you should know."

Kelly stared at him, then turned and glared. Her look of hatred burned into Jenny's soul. "How... could... you!" she howled.

Ryan was still clueless, his worry overshadowing his normally sharp deductive skills. "How could she what?"

Dan spoke up. "Ryan, we're in love. It wasn't planned, it just happened."

Ryan shook his head. "What the..."

"You fucking bitch!" Kelly screeched, lunging at her. Dan stood in the way to prevent any contact from being made.

Jenny cringed and backed away from her now ex-best friend. She understood this was the price she had to pay for loving Dan and she found it hurt too much. "Kelly, I didn't mean to. I'm sorry!"

"Don't give me that shit. You are my best friend, Jenny. No. You *were* my best friend!" Kelly turned back on Dan and started hitting him viciously on the chest. "You motherfucker! How could you do this to me?" Dan stood there and took her blows without defending himself. It appeared he was taking her punishment gratefully, as if he wanted Kelly to hit him.

Ryan did not react the same way. He looked at Jenny with tears in his eyes. "It was a stupid fling. This was all a mistake. I don't believe for a second that you love him. Let me take you home and we can work this out." Jenny had expected him to fly off the handle; instead, he was trying to fix it. It was one of Ryan's most endearing qualities.

"Oh, Rye," she whimpered. She looked at the love reflected in his eyes and felt a wave of regret. He took her hand and led her out of the cabin towards his car. Jenny resisted at first, but part of her wanted to run away from the painful encounter.

"Don't," Dan called out. She looked back, drawn to him like a magnet. His blond hair covered his eyes, but he didn't sweep it back as he waited for her decision. "Don't leave me, Jenny." Her heart contracted. Although her love for him was new, it was intense—unlike anything she'd felt before. Jenny stopped in her tracks, ready to fight for him... until she looked into the eyes of her best friend.

The hate radiating from Kelly was palpable. "Get out of here, bitch!" she snarled. Jenny could see the severe pain her actions had caused etched in Kelly's face and it shattered her resolve to stay.

Ryan pulled on her arm. She looked one last time at Dan, tears welling up in her eyes. She couldn't do it. She couldn't hurt them any more than she already had. Jenny reluctantly followed Ryan out of the cabin and out of Dan's life.

This love was doomed from the start... Jenny thought, as she stared out the window of the car while they drove away. Smoke drifted up out of the chimney, beckoning her to come back—to revel in the warmth she had enjoyed alone in the snowbound cabin with Dan.

Ryan pulled Jenny out of her daze with a pointed question. "I have to know. Did you really fuck Dan?"

As bad as it was, she was determined not to make it worse by lying. "We did everything *but* traditional fucking."

Ryan turned his head towards her with a raised eyebrow. "You kept your pussy away from him?"

She blushed. How much was too much information? She added softly, "He took me anally, Rye."

Jenny didn't miss the shudder when he replied, "Dan did you that way? I guess when you're desperate…"

She ignored the feeling of rejection his shudder wrought. Ryan was grossed-out by massaging her feet, so the idea of taking her anally was way beyond his comfort level. It would have been easy to let him think it ended there, but he deserved to know the whole truth.

"Ryan, I was going to make love to him today."

"But you didn't," he said, slamming his hands down on the steering wheel, "because I came and rescued you in time."

"Ryan…"

"No, this was just a set of unfortunate circumstances. You do not love Dan. *We* are more important than five days spent in a cabin."

She leaned against the window. In typical Ryan fashion, he'd already found a logical way to handle the situation. It was simply a mistake; it was not going to change their relationship. She sighed.

Until she knew what was happening between Kelly and Dan, this was the easiest route to take. If those two stayed together, there was no point in breaking up with Ryan. Even though he didn't compare to Dan, he was a good guy.

Better than I deserve.

When Ryan arrived at their apartment, he took her by the hand and led her inside. She was hesitant to enter, suddenly feeling queasy.

He smiled at her. "I am glad to have you back home where you belong. I have missed you, Jenny Boo." His use of her college nickname softened her heart. He'd given it to her at a Halloween party shortly after they met. Ryan grazed his hand against her cheek lovingly. He made it easy to slip back into the way things were. Maybe he was right; a string of chance circumstances had ignited an unusual situation. In the real world, the love affair would never have happened.

The two spent a quiet evening together. Ryan cooked a simple meal and kept the conversation light. When it came time for bed, he started undressing and said huskily, "I want to be close to you tonight." Jenny felt she owed it to Ryan and began stripping off her clothes. It would ease the guilt of being unfaithful.

Ryan pulled her to him, kissing her firmly on the lips. "*My* Jenny," he growled as he kissed her neck and cradled her breasts in both hands. He worshipped her breasts. Jenny threw her head back and let him suckle them. It was one thing that Ryan really dug and she appreciated his attention.

Sadly, the way he handled foreplay reminded her of a business transaction. It was quick and to the point, never lasting long enough. Soon he was pushing her against the bed with his body weight. She fell back onto it, giving into his need—wanting to feel connected to him again, *needing* to feel that this was the right thing for her.

Ryan thrust his hard shaft into her without any undue ceremony. He grabbed her hips and began stroking her with his lengthy cock. "I love you, Jenny. Nothing else matters." He was staking his claim after the affair. She instinctually understood that this was his way of preserving his manhood. She opened herself to him and allowed Ryan deep inside.

He fucked her for literally an hour. She was tempted to play with her clit to help herself orgasm, but doing something new would only highlight the fact she had been with another man. She resisted the urge, letting Ryan have his way with her body. She could tell he was proud of himself for lasting so long, but the reality of it was that her insides were sore by the time he finally grunted out his climax.

"This… is… for… you!" he cried, as his dick rammed into her forcefully to finish off the session.

She echoed his cry in a pretend orgasm. "Oh, Rye, yes, yes!" She knew he wouldn't be satisfied unless he pleased her and, after an hour, all she wanted was rest. She curled up in a ball afterwards with tears in her eyes. This was what she had signed up for—a good man and minimal pleasure. Until Dan, she hadn't realized it could be any other way.

The next morning she tried to contact him from

her office. Dan didn't answer his cell or his work phone. She called throughout the day, but it appeared he had cut off all contact from her. After a week of trying to reach him, she finally gave up. Either Kelly had instructed him not to have anything to do with her or Dan hadn't forgiven her for leaving him behind.

The unresolved feelings she had for the man haunted her constantly. She tried to continue forward with Ryan, but everything felt different. She still loved Rye, but Jenny realized that she had never been *in love* with him.

She was completely and utterly in love with Dan. Just thinking about him gave her butterflies. She longed to hear his deep voice, to feel his warm caresses, to smell his musky scent. Everything about him was desirable and perfect. To be away from that, to be forced to live life without his presence was like a partial death. She knew she would never be whole again.

After another quiet dinner together, Ryan gave her a sympathetic look. "What's wrong, Boo?"

She had been thinking of Dan and glanced at him, her cheeks burning red with guilt. "Nothing."

"Don't tell me *nothing*. I can see it in your eyes. You're clearly suffering."

"It's not important."

"I disagree. It's important if it is causing you pain."

Jenny sighed heavily, not able to look him in the eye when she answered. "You don't want to hear my thoughts, trust me."

He put his fork down. "Are you thinking of Dan?"

Tears came to her eyes when she whispered, "Yes."

"I talked to him today," Ryan announced as he got up from the table and cleared away the dishes. Jenny tried to hide her interest, but he saw right through her and added, "Yes, Dan seems to be as miserable as you are."

"Oh," she murmured, both happy and upset to hear that he was suffering as well.

"Kelly dumped him that day at the cabin. He's been staying with a coworker while he tries to find a place, but you know how that is. Cheap apartments are impossible to come by in this city, especially on short notice."

Jenny gazed intensely at Ryan, trying to read between the lines. Why was he telling her this? What was his hidden agenda? "I agree. Finding a place won't be easy for him," she responded guardedly.

He stared at her without speaking. It appeared he was trying to build the courage to say something important. She waited patiently while he scraped the plates, and then washed his hands before returning to the table. "Boo, you should know that I told Dan not to contact you."

Jenny felt a surge of anger, immediately followed by a wave of guilt. Of course he had the right to do that. She'd cheated on him. Jenny would do no less if it were the other way around.

He continued, "I must admit, I appreciate the fact Dan has honored my request." Jenny nodded her head, unsure what he expected her to say.

Ryan took her hand and held it in his. "I want you to be happy, Jen. I don't like seeing you like this." She was moved by the love expressed in his luminous green eyes. He was the opposite of Dan in his features. He had short dark brown curls, emeralds for eyes, and a lean build. There was no doubt that Ryan loved her and she still loved him—even if it wasn't the "fireworks" kind of love she felt for Dan.

Ryan kissed the back of her hand tenderly and said, "Don't give up on me yet."

Jenny gave him a weak smile. "You have been so understanding, Rye. I don't deserve it."

"I would disagree," he answered.

Why did Ryan have to be so sweet? It actually hurt her heart that he was being so kind.

"I love you, Jenny. More than you know." He leaned over and kissed her lightly on the lips.

She went to bed that night thinking about Dan. Knowing that he wanted to be with her was pure torture. Still, Jenny couldn't leave Ryan. The simple truth was that she loved him enough to keep trying.

Ryan's Gift

Ryan shocked Jenny when he called her at work the next day and told her to meet him at the Oxford hotel at six. He was a self-professed workaholic. Late nights at the office were common, but leaving at a reasonable hour on a weekday was *not*. As if he could read her thoughts, he said, "I want to change things up a little, Jen. I'm determined to see that beautiful smile on your face tonight. Let's meet in the lobby. I have a special surprise for you."

Jenny couldn't help it, she squealed in excitement. "You know how much I love surprises!"

"I do, and I promise this is something you'll never guess."

"Do I get a hint?"

"Nope."

"You are a cruel man, Rye."

He laughed softly. "Tonight marks a new chapter in our lives." Jenny thought she heard a nervous sigh on the other end of the line. What could Ryan have in mind that would make him so anxious? It had her extremely curious—even a little amorous, and made waiting until the end of the work day a challenge.

Jenny arrived fifteen minutes early, anxious to discover his surprise. She was tickled by the gently falling snow when she stepped out of her car. The flakes were enchanting against the backdrop of the historic hotel.

Ryan was already waiting for her inside near the center statue. His face lit up when he saw her, but he was fidgeting with the change in his pocket. His nerves hit her from clear across the large foyer. The way Ryan was acting reminded her of their first date. Jenny glided over to him and smiled reassuringly. "Hi, stranger."

"Hello, beautiful. Are you ready for the biggest surprise of your life?"

The thought he might propose came to mind and she suddenly felt panicky. There was no way she was ready for that.

Ryan read the concern on her face and wrapped his arms around her. "Don't worry. I'm sure you'll like it. It's up in our room, in fact."

Jenny giggled in nervous relief. Okay, he was simply planning to have a sexy interlude. *That* she could handle. "Well, what are we waiting for?" She grabbed his hand and headed for the elevator, but Ryan hesitated for a second.

Jenny could feel his tension and was reminded again of their first date together. What could have him so spooked? Now her curiosity was royally piqued!

When they reached the room, he took her hand and squeezed it tightly. His palm was clammy. Jenny looked into his eyes, trying to figure him out. "Whatever it is, Rye, I'm sure I will like it. You don't have to be so worried."

Ryan's cheeks flushed before he kissed her. "I'm suddenly afraid you might like it too much."

The suspense was killing her. "There is only one way to find out," she said with a wink. Ryan slipped the card in and opened the door for her. Jenny walked through the doorway and froze.

"Hi, Jenny." Dan stood in front of her with a crooked little grin.

She couldn't move even though her body longed to rush into Dan's arms. Jenny looked at Ryan apprehensively. "What's going on?"

Nervous laughter filled the room. "I... Well, we both love you. I have been talking to Dan all week. I think I've figured out a way for all of us to be happy."

She stared at him in astonishment.

Dan spoke up. "We both want to please you tonight."

She didn't realize she'd stopped breathing until her lungs complained. Jenny gasped for air, afraid she might faint.

Ryan put his arm around her. "Are you okay, Jen? I thought you would be happy."

Jenny looked at him and then back to Dan. *This*

is too much!

"I think she's in shock, Ryan. Give her a few minutes." Dan walked over to the desk and picked up two glasses. "I mixed some drinks for us." He came over and handed her one. When Jenny grabbed the stem of the glass, Dan brushed his hand over hers. Her whole body tingled from the simple contact.

Dan gave the other glass to Ryan and then retrieved the last one for himself. He took a sip and smiled. "A damn good martini, if I say so myself."

Jenny took a taste. It didn't live up to hers. "It'll do."

Dan snorted. "Perfectionist."

"Amateur."

Ryan took his own sip. "Jenny makes a better drink."

"Et tu, Brute?" Dan complained.

Jenny relaxed hearing the familiar banter. They had been best friends for over three years. Being together again felt good. She took another long sip and then smiled at Ryan. "Thank you."

"You're okay with this then?"

She smiled shyly. "What girl wouldn't want two gorgeous men?"

Ryan cupped her chin. "I was hoping to see that smile again. I told you I loved you more than you knew."

"I never appreciated how much." Jenny kissed him, giggling nervously.

Dan moved closer to her and put his hand on

the small of her back. She could barely breathe when she felt the warmth of his touch. "That makes two of us who love you." He leaned down and kissed her on the lips right in front of Ryan. Her knees gave under her. Luckily, Dan had his arm around her before she collapsed and she only spilled a little of her drink.

This isn't real...

"So, I want to lay down some ground rules first," Ryan announced. "Jenny's pussy is all mine. No different than when you guys were alone together." Jenny was surprised, but wasn't about to complain. Dan nodded his head, as if the two had already discussed it. "Also, there's no male-to-male touching."

Dan frowned. "Like I would want to touch any part of you."

"I just needed to make that perfectly clear." Ryan added with a grin, "I've seen the way you look at me."

Dan snorted. "In your dreams."

Jenny's heart rate increased as she observed the two men ribbing each other. She was about to have sex with both of them at the same time: the two men she loved most in the world. It felt so decadent, so wrong—but oh so exciting.

Ryan started unbuttoning his shirt and tossed it to the ground. When he went to unbuckle his belt, Dan protested. "What are you doing, man?"

Ryan looked at Dan questioningly. "What?"

"Where's the romance in just throwing clothes

off?"

Ryan crinkled his brow. "We're having sex, not a fashion show."

"May I?" Dan asked, glancing towards Jenny. When Ryan nodded his acquiescence, he walked over to her and lifted her chin. He kissed her passionately as he unbuttoned her blouse.

Jenny's heart beat a mile a minute as he pulled the material away and let it fall to the floor. "Beautiful and amusing," he murmured, kissing her left shoulder while he reached around and undid her smiley face bra. It was the next thing to go. Jenny burned with embarrassment. This was the second time he'd caught her wearing the comfortable but ancient bra.

Ryan returned to her side. "I'll do the rest."

Dan moved to her left to give Ryan room. While he unbuttoned her jeans, Dan cupped her breast and bent down to lick her nipple. Jenny felt a gush of wetness soak her panties. The attention of both men was almost *too* intense.

Ryan wrestled her jeans to the ground. Jenny smelled her own excitement wafting up from between her legs. Dan smelled it, too. "Oh, you do like this, don't you?" he growled in her ear.

Ryan pulled her panties off next. "Wow, I've never seen you this wet before, Jenny."

The heat rose to her cheeks. It was disconcerting not to be able to hide how excited she was. She was afraid that it would upset Ryan, but he seemed to enjoy it. He planted a kiss on her dark mound before standing up again.

She stood there completely naked while Dan still had all his clothes on and Ryan only had his shirt off. Jenny turned to Ryan first and undid his belt. She knelt down and kissed his abdomen as she tugged at his pants and helped him out of them. His erection was quite evident under the thin material of his jockeys. She slowly pulled them off as well, kissing his cock in the process. His dick was already rock hard and warm from so much blood flowing through it. It jerked when her lips touched the smooth head of his cock. Jenny could tell he was as turned on as she was, which only excited her more.

Jenny stood up and faced Dan next. She lifted his shirt but was too short to pull it over his head. He helped her remove it, chuckling lightly. His chest with its blond curls was just as handsome as she remembered. She was tempted to make a joke about strip poker, but didn't want Ryan to feel left out. Instead, she just smiled to herself and undid his jeans. They pooled down around his ankles.

Jenny looked up at Dan as she gingerly removed his boxers next. His eyes reflected both love and lust in equal amounts. She glanced at his cock and was pleased to see a large drop of precome on the end of his thick member. She stuck her tongue out and licked it, tasting his tangy essence. He grunted, which made her loins contract in pleasure. All she wanted was to feel Dan deep inside her again. It was apparent that his cock wanted the same thing.

"Dan, let's take her to the bed. I want to feel

those lips wrapped around my dick," Ryan growled.

He held out his hand and helped Jenny to her feet. She walked over to the bed and lay down on her back with her head near the edge. Ryan moved to her head and eased his cock into her mouth as he stroked the remainder of his long thin shaft. Meanwhile, Dan settled down between her legs and began licking her pussy. Her body reacted eagerly to his tongue and her loins ignited the instant his talented mouth met her sensitive clit. She moaned as he sucked and flicked with precision.

Jenny took Ryan's shaft deeper into her mouth in response to the sexual energy Dan was generating. Ryan gasped in surprise and pleasure. "Oh my God, Jenny. You've gotten better at that!" He grabbed onto her head and thrust his cock further into her mouth. Jenny was concentrating solely on sucking Ryan until she felt Dan's fingers begin to stroke her wet outer lips. She stiffened when he penetrated her with his finger. She was unsure if it was allowed, but Ryan didn't seem to care. He was focused on his cock disappearing into her mouth.

Jenny moaned around Ryan's cock as Dan explored her pussy with his fingers for the first time. It felt so naughty. She felt her entire groin contract when he stroked his finger deep inside her velvety tunnel. He continued stroking her there, making her cry out and then gasp as another powerful contraction overtook her.

Ryan pulled away from her mouth and asked, "What's going on?"

"I'm stroking her G-spot. It appears that Jenny likes it," Dan answered huskily.

She yelped as another contraction sent a wave of electricity through her. Ryan watched in fascination as Jenny squirmed and whimpered under Dan's focused touch. When he placed his warm lips back on her clit and started sucking, her whole body stiffened.

Jenny had never been stimulated that way before and had no control over the orgasm advancing on her. "Oh shit!" she moaned just before a huge wave of concentrated pleasure enveloped her. Her pussy pushed up against Dan's lips without her permission. She had no control as her hips lifted off the bed in a rhythmic motion. When the climax finally ended, Jenny shuddered and lay limp on the bed, whimpering softly.

"What was that? I've *never* seen Jenny do that before."

"It's her G-spot, man. Haven't you played with it before?" Dan asked, looking up from between her legs.

"No," Ryan answered, sounding lost and a bit defensive.

Jenny took pity on him. "Come here, Rye." She took hold of his cock and guided it back into her mouth. She wiggled her tongue against the ridge of his silky head and then took him deep into her mouth again. He looked down at her lustfully, apparently enjoying the erotic sight of his shaft thrusting in and out of her rosy pink lips, but it proved too much. "I can't take anymore. I know what my cock really needs. Move out of the way, Dan."

Ryan climbed onto the bed and positioned himself between her legs. He pushed his rigid cock deep into her swollen pussy. "Oh yeah, now that's what I am talking about!"

Dan bent over and began kissing her breasts, nibbling and licking them randomly as he lightly kneaded her nipples between his fingers. Then Dan moved up to her ear and whispered, "You are so sexy, Jenny. I loved how you came around my finger just now."

She groaned at the memory of the orgasm. It was the first time he had touched her like that and she'd loved every minute of it. The head of Ryan's cock began rubbing against the same area Dan had stimulated. "Oh Rye, that feels *really* good. Keep fucking me just like that."

His strokes came faster and harder as he tried to please her. "Come for me, Boo. I want to feel you come as hard for me as you did for Dan."

Jenny threw her head back and moaned. Then she grabbed Dan's thick shaft. She licked and lightly teethed his cock, wanting to bring him to the edge with her. "I want to taste your come, Dan. I want it to fill my mouth." Ryan had denied her his come and she wasn't about to let Dan do the same.

She matched Ryan's strokes inside her with her own movements on Dan's shaft. The three were in sync—it was a beautiful thing. A cold chill crawled over her body, making her nipples ache and her groin contract. A second climax was close at hand.

Jenny pulled her lips away for a moment. "Dan, are you close?" He nodded his head, grunting softly. "Good, so am I. Try to come with me." She slipped his cock back into her mouth and started sucking hard and fast. Jenny pushed against each stroke of Ryan's shaft, launching him deep into her quivering pussy. After several mind-blowing thrusts, Jenny's muffled cries filled the hotel room as she came around Ryan's solid manhood.

The minute she started crying out in pleasure, Dan's cock stiffened and then released a flood of hot semen. Jenny eagerly swallowed his seed, loving the power she had to make him climax so easily.

Ryan was still fucking her hard when her second orgasm ended. He looked down at Jenny with a huge grin. "That felt fucking fantastic!" He quickly pulled out and told her to get on her hands and knees. Doggy style was Ryan's favorite position. She arched her back for him as his long dick hammered her needy depths. The new angle felt amazing for them both.

Jenny started screaming when he grabbed her waist and thrust his entire length into her. There were times his shaft was too long, but this was definitely not one of them. Her body wanted all he could give her and more.

"Oh yeah, you take it. You take all of my cock!" Ryan shouted. Jenny had never seen him so excited in bed. He rarely lost control in any situation, business or personal. Having Dan there seemed to bring out a completely new side to her man.

"I want to feel you come inside me, Rye," she moaned.

Instantly, his strokes increased in tempo. For the first time in ages, Ryan allowed himself to let go completely. "Here is it! I'm creaming you on the inside just like you asked." He grunted as his buttocks flexed, shoving his cock deep.

She cried out at the depth of his penetration. "I love it! I love it!" she gasped.

Both collapsed on the bed after his climax. She thought she heard giggling out in the hallway. She looked up at Dan with a worried expression. Jenny hadn't even thought to be quiet. The entire hotel had probably heard their lovemaking.

Dan grinned wickedly. "They're just jealous."

After a few minutes, Ryan lifted himself off the bed and went to wash himself. Once he was thoroughly clean, he started to dress. "I'm starving! Let's go get something to eat."

Jenny rolled lazily onto her stomach. "Are you serious?"

He looked at her with a deadpan face. "Of course. A fuck like that demands sustenance, especially if we plan to do more."

Jenny couldn't believe her ears. "More?"

Dan lightly stroked her long black hair down the length of her back. "I haven't come inside you yet."

Her whole body trembled at the thought. She longed to be filled up with Dan while in Ryan's loving embrace. It gave her pleasant butterflies just to think of it.

It Should be Illegal

Jenny cleaned up and took special care to apply her makeup. She wanted to look good for her two men. They left the room arm in arm with Jenny in the middle. It garnered the stares of several people on their way down. What did Jenny care? She was in heaven.

The threesome was given a booth in the corner of the crowded restaurant. Jenny looked around and noticed an uptight woman staring at them judgmentally. Jenny giggled at her and then kissed Dan passionately. Jenny looked back at the old woman before turning to Ryan and cupping his face in her hands. She kissed him long and deep, taking her time. When she broke away, Jenny noticed the old lady nudging her husband with a look of disbelief.

Dan seemed amused by her little game and grabbed her by the waist, pulling her onto his lap. He nuzzled her neck. "You're a bad girl, aren't you?"

"Bad in a good way," she answered, biting his ear playfully.

Ryan interrupted them. "Decide what you want to eat, because we need to order. I'm starving."

Dan kissed Jenny gently on the lips. "Feel free to eat anything on the menu. Garlic, onions, none of it will faze us."

Ryan held out his arms to her, so Jenny moved over into his lap. "Speak for yourself, bub." He nibbled on her ear and mumbled, "Jenny knows I hate the taste of garlic."

She gave Ryan a pretty little pout. "But I wanted the garlic chicken tonight, dear."

"Come on, Ryan. Don't be such a control freak. Let the girl order what she wants," Dan said, giving Jenny a tweak on the nose.

Ryan grumbled, "Okay, fine. Order the damn chicken."

Jenny laughed sweetly as she wrapped her arms around him. "I was just kidding anyway. What I really want is the onion burger with a side of blue cheese."

Ryan rolled his eyes and pushed her off him. "Get away from me, woman."

"Come back to me, my little kumquat," said Dan, gathering her into his arms. "There is absolutely nothing you could eat that would make any part of you taste bad." He ran his tongue lightly over her lips. "So yummy..." Jenny's insides quaked from his attention.

While they were engaged with one another, the

waiter came up. Ryan ordered three garlic chickens and the onion burger with an extra large helping of blue cheese on the side. He smiled at them both. "Hah! Now we all will taste disgusting."

"You do realize I hate onions," Dan informed him.

"Too bad, sucker. We both get to suffer."

"I bet I can get you boys to like it," Jenny replied confidently.

Dan looked amused. "Oh really?"

Jenny spent the dinner feeding both men seductively, forkful by sensual forkful. By the time she was done, most of the restaurant was watching the three. Dan lightly caressed her cheek. She happened to glance down and notice the hard-on straining in his pants.

"Are you ready for me to take you?" he asked, making her loins tingle pleasurably.

Ryan leaned into her, pressing his own erection against her thigh. "Maybe I can practice playing with your G-spot."

Jenny whispered in his ear, "I can't wait."

The men escorted her out of the restaurant, walking a little stiffer than when they came in. It made Jenny giggle. *What a scandalous threesome we are!*

Dan unlocked their room and gestured her inside. "The lady first." He closed the door behind them and slid the lock into place. She looked at him, unable to hide the excitement she felt, but wanting everything to be perfect. "Wait a sec. Give me just a couple of minutes." She disappeared in the bathroom to take a quick shower. Jenny was just lathering up when both men entered the tiny bathroom.

"What do you think you are doing?" Dan asked.

She peeked from behind the curtain. "I just wanted to freshen up before the next round."

"Without us?" Ryan accused.

A smile spread across her face. "Well, if you two want to join me you're more than welcome."

Both men stepped into the small tub. There was hardly any room to move, but it didn't seem to matter. Ryan and Dan were content to lather her body in suds, rubbing their hands all over her breasts and between her legs. She felt it only fair and lathered up both of their cocks simultaneously. The soap made them extremely slippery and fun to play with, but her men wouldn't let her play for long. Instead, Ryan patted her dry while Dan got things ready in the bedroom.

Jenny was a little nervous about taking Dan anally in front of Ryan. Not only was he a bit of a germophobe, but he was about to witness Jenny being fucked by another man. "Rye?"

He looked up from the floor where he was drying her calves. "Yeah?"

"Are you sure you can handle this?"

He stopped what he was doing. Ryan stood up and gazed into her eyes. "I am not sure how well I will handle my best friend taking pleasure in you. But it's been fun so far, so I am willing to try."

She wrapped her arms around him. Ryan had given so much of himself by arranging this threesome. He totally meant it when he said he loved her. In every way, Ryan had proved it tonight. "I really love you, Rye," she whispered.

He pressed his forehead against hers. "I love you, Boo."

"What's going on in there?" Dan called out from the bedroom.

Ryan squeezed her hand and led her to the bed. "None of your business, big shot."

Dan looked at Jenny questioningly. She just smiled and walked over to him, kissing him innocently. He grasped the back of her neck and slipped his tongue into her mouth. He grazed against her teeth before darting his tongue in further. How could Dan make her desperate for him with just a simple kiss? Ryan was probably asking the same question. To Jenny, it was as if Dan was an addictive drug, something her body craved and couldn't get enough of.

"If you don't mind, Ryan, I want to give her a quick massage before we get started."

"By all means," he answered, "as long as I can join in."

"Whatever pleases the lady," Dan replied. He started at her feet, the same way he had the last time. However, before caressing her with his magic fingers he kissed each of her toes. "Jenny has the tastiest toes."

"I'll have to trust you on that," Ryan stated blandly.

"You don't know what you're missing, man," he

countered. Jenny closed her eyes and enjoyed the experience of Dan nibbling and licking her toes. It seemed so sinful, especially since Ryan hated feet. The sensation tickled and made her squirm, but it also sent tiny shock waves to her groin.

Jenny let out a grateful sigh when he began the deep massage. Dan pressed his fingers into her muscles, drawing out weeks of pent-up tension. While he caressed her body, Ryan whispered in her ear, "I love pleasing you, Jenny." Ryan nuzzled her ear playfully and then squeezed and sucked on her nipples. "I also love these gorgeous breasts of yours."

Jenny smiled. *Aw… my breast man.*

Dan shifted on the bed and announced, "Baby, I'm ready if you are." Her heart skipped a beat hearing Dan call her "baby" in front of Ryan and she wondered how it made Ryan feel.

Jenny kissed Ryan on the lips to reassure him before answering Dan. "Yes, I am quite relaxed and ready."

She got on her hands and knees, her body weak with desire for him. She bit her bottom lip when she felt the cold gel touch the crease of her ass. Dan spread it around liberally and then slowly penetrated her puckered hole with his slippery index finger. She took a quick peek at Ryan and saw him watching intently with no expression on his face.

Jenny looked back at Dan as he coated his thick cock in the lubricant. It was so different doing it in the hotel with Ryan observing them, but it added an element of excitement, too. Making love to Dan with Ryan's full permission was a dream come true. She felt ready to burst with love for them both.

The mattress shifted as Dan got ready to take her. She felt rather than saw Ryan stiffen, but he remained silent. Dan's hands danced over her back while he pressed the head of his cock against her tight hole. For a second she tensed, until his fingers slid down between her legs and Dan began playing with her throbbing clit. Jenny moaned softly and began pushing against his shaft. It slid in easier than it had the first time and she gasped.

"Is he hurting you?" Ryan demanded.

Jenny shook her head. "No. It feels good." She arched her back more and pushed his cock in deeper.

Dan started groaning low and deep. "You feel so tight, Jenny. I can hardly stand how good it feels."

"I know," moaned Jenny, "it's sooo good."

Dan put his hands on her hips and began shallow thrusts. She squealed in pleasure and then looked at Ryan guiltily.

His lips were pressed together so firmly that the outer part was ringed in white, but his eyes were glazed over with lust. She looked down and saw that his cock was rock hard. Even if this was difficult for him, Ryan was definitely turned on by it.

Jenny closed her eyes and moaned a little louder. "Deeper. I need it deeper."

Dan readily complied and she soon felt his full

strokes caressing her insides. He grabbed a fistful of her long black hair and pulled it back gently. Jenny was surprised to feel Ryan's warm lips press against her mouth. It was so erotic having him kiss her while Dan took her in the ass and she felt the first stirrings of an orgasm. "Ryan, touch my clit. I'm so close to coming."

He reached down and rubbed it awkwardly. She put her hand on his and showed him the pace and pressure she needed. Jenny put her hand back down to brace herself against Dan's thrusts. "Oh yes! So good, so fucking good!" she cried.

Both men groaned at the same time, Dan above her and Ryan in her mouth, while her body shivered in ecstasy. Jenny screamed when her climax hit. Dan pushed harder and started coming deep inside her ass. Ryan grabbed onto his cock and stroked himself vigorously. Thick white liquid shot out of his shaft, landing on the bed. He grunted as he came, it was a beautiful sight. Jenny had never known Ryan to come twice in one night—ever.

She leaned over and licked the come off the tip of his shaft. "You don't have to do that," Ryan said, trying to pull away.

Jenny held onto his cock and told him, "I want to." She sucked on his creamy cock until it was clean. He shuddered after she was done. Normally, a shudder from him meant disgust, but the look of satisfaction on Ryan's face spoke volumes.

Dan slowly pulled out of her and kissed the small of her back. "You have the sexiest body, woman. I can't seem to get enough of it."

The three of them lay on the bed in silence, relaxing in the pleasant afterglow.

"Dan?"

"Yes, Ryan," Dan said with a contented drawl.

"Would you be interested in doing this again over the weekend?"

His answer was quick. "Absolutely."

Jenny propped up her head and stared at both of them. "Don't I get a say?"

Ryan retorted, "Like you would say no."

She lay back down and smiled. "True."

Ryan stared at the ceiling and said offhandedly, "There are a few things I'd like to try." Jenny felt her loins burn with anticipation. Ryan wanted to try new things? *Be still, my beating heart.* "Would Saturday night work for you?" he asked Dan.

"Of course," Dan replied, smiling at Jenny.

"Good." Ryan got up and walked to the bathroom.

While he was gone Jenny asked in a low whisper, "Dan, why are you here?"

He turned and looked at her questioningly. "What do you mean?"

"This has got to be hard for you."

He cupped her chin. "Jenny, I love you. I would do anything to be with you, even if it means sharing you with my best friend."

Tears filled her eyes. "It's not fair to either of you."

He brushed the tear from her cheek. "We are

both grown men. No one is forcing us to do this."

When Ryan came out of the bathroom, she quickly kissed Dan and mouthed, "Thank you."

Ryan returned with a huge grin on his face. "I don't think I have ever had so much fun in one night. This should be illegal."

"Probably is," Dan joked.

Ryan plopped on the bed, making them both bounce as he landed. He looked more relaxed than she'd ever seen him. She placed her hand on his smooth chest and stared into his emerald eyes. "Thank you, Ryan."

His voice was laced with tenderness. "I love you, Jen."

She scooted next to Ryan and kissed him on the lips. "I love you too."

Ryan looked over at Dan and nodded to Jenny. "You can tell him how you feel. I don't mind."

She gazed at Dan, adoring the look of his tousled blond hair and boyish grin. "I love you too, Dan."

Dan threw open his arms and she crawled into them. He leaned his chin on top of her head as they embraced. She looked over at Ryan, grateful to see him smiling.

The three left shortly after. Each drove home in their separate vehicles even though Jenny was meeting Ryan at their apartment. Alone in her car, Jenny marveled at the fact that two men loved her so completely. It didn't seem possible—she felt unbelievably cherished.

Poor Kelly…

New Ventures

Jenny made the mistake of trying to contact her ex-best friend during her lunch hour. Kelly hadn't taken her phone calls, so she resorted to visiting her at work. As Jenny walked towards the towering glass building she was overcome by a feeling of dread and she almost turned back, but her determination won out. This was her best friend; their friendship was worth whatever Kelly would require to repair it.

The receptionist escorted Jenny to Kelly's cubicle, but the instant she entered, Kelly screeched, "Get the hell out of my office. How dare you come here!"

"I just want to talk."

Kelly's face turned a dark color of crimson before she burst into a torrent of curse words. "Why the hell would I want to talk to a backstabbing, cocksucking whore of a bitch!"

Several people popped their heads up to watch the show play out. Jenny looked at Kelly in desperation, not wanting it to end like this. "Please, let's go somewhere private to talk."

"No! I don't want to have anything to do with you or that pussy-whipped fucker. You can go to hell!"

"I never meant to hurt you, Kelly."

"Shut the fuck up! Don't even go there, you... you... fucking *cunt!*"

Jenny shrank from the venom spewing out of her best friend. "I'm sorry. I'm so sorry..." The last of her courage had evaporated, so she turned and ran out of the office.

What the hell was I thinking? There was no way to repair the friendship she'd decimated. Jenny sped off in her car and proceeded to get a traffic ticket two blocks away. "Do you know how fast you were going, miss?"

She looked up at the officer, tears streaming down her face, and sniffled, "No..."

"Fifteen miles over the posted speed limit," he answered curtly.

"I'm sorry," she sobbed. "I'm just so sorry."

The cop spent the next ten minutes trying to calm her down. It wasn't until he threatened to call an ambulance that she gained control of herself. "It's a hundred-dollar fine. You can pay it via mail or show up at your assigned court date. My sugges-tion," he offered, "don't drive when you are upset. It's not safe for you *or* the other drivers."

Jenny nodded her head and started crying again. The officer quickly walked to his car and drove off.

She stayed there a full hour, hating herself for betraying her friend. Kelly was right, she *was* a backstabbing bitch. She recalled the look on Kelly's face at the cabin the moment she realized what they had done. It stabbed at Jenny's heart.

Immediately, another memory flitted through her mind—the time in Jamaica when the boys had gone off scuba diving while Kelly and she stayed on the beach and took turns burying each other in the sand. It took days before Jenny got all the grit out of her intimate crevices, but damn, she had never laughed so hard in her life. Kelly had a unique ability to make her feel like a kid again, it was something Jenny had always loved about her.

And now their friendship was dead. Jenny had seen to that with her infidelity. She laid her head on the steering wheel and let out a deep, aching sob. She had to face the cold, hard reality—even if she could turn back time, she wouldn't change a thing. She loved Dan *and* Ryan. Despite all the pain she had caused Kelly, being loved by both men was truly a gift. If she was completely honest, it was worth losing her friendship with Kelly.

I'm going to hell, she thought as she turned on her car and headed back to work.

Jenny wasn't planning to tell anyone about her failed attempt to reconcile. Sadly, her ex-best friend was not as discreet. Dan called her in the afternoon. "I heard you tried to smooth things over with Kelly."

She felt a large sob forming in her throat and

had to swallow it down. "Yeah, stupid, I know."

"I could have told you it wasn't worth it, Jenny. Why did you even try?"

"She's my best friend," Jenny whimpered.

"No, you thought she was your best friend. Kelly is only friend to one person—herself."

"That's not fair, Dan. We betrayed her, the two people she trusted most in the world."

"Jenny, I don't know how much truth you can handle. Although she hid it, Kelly grew to resent you. You are everything she is not."

"But that's not true. Kelly is one of the funnest people I know."

"That may be, but I lived with the woman 24/7. I know a different side to her. What Kelly presents to the world is a facade. Underneath her *playfulness* lies a hurting child. To be honest, she reminds me of her father."

"But that crazy bastard ruined her life... and her mother's." Jenny hated the man for all the devastation he had caused while Kelly was growing up and she protested loudly, "She's not anything like that man!"

Dan let out a long sigh. "I understand, Jenny. Until you see it for yourself, you can't imagine the anger she hides and what she is capable of. I've often wondered if it's her genes and she's just naturally crazy, or if the divorce damaged her beyond repair. Whatever the case, Kelly has issues. Deep issues. I really wish you hadn't contacted her."

"Why, Dan? What did she say to you?"

"What was said is between her and I. But take my advice; stay away from her—for both our sakes."

Jenny didn't want to cause Ryan to worry, so she chose not to say anything when she got home. Instead, she focused on the sensual possibilities Saturday night promised for the three of them. She was curious what Ryan wanted to try in the bedroom, but he refused to tell her.

However, he did spend time attempting to find her G-spot, hoping to make her come like she had at the hotel. Unfortunately, try as he might, Ryan couldn't locate it and she was absolutely no help. Jenny found it amusing that Dan seemed to know her body better than she did.

For Saturday's big event, Jenny took extra time primping. She covered herself in lilac-scented lotion and picked out her prettiest satin bra and panty set. Jenny threw her ancient bra in the trash. *No more smiley faces for me.* She finished the look by creating soft strands of black curls to frame her face. When she came out of the bedroom, Ryan whistled. "You've never looked more beautiful, Boo."

She wrapped her arms around his waist and kissed him lightly on the lips. "Love will do that to a person."

Ryan had chosen a different hotel for their second rendezvous, one that was known as a romantic get-away for couples with its large brass beds and free champagne. He worried that they'd made enough noise at the Oxford that they might not to be welcomed back.

Jenny took his hand and squeezed it when the elevator doors opened to their floor. "Ready for another night of incredible sex?" he growled hoarsely.

"Always." Jenny was a bundle of nerves. Even though they had done this once before, the fact that Ryan wanted to try new things had her quivering in anticipation.

Jenny's heart fluttered when the hotel door opened and she saw Dan standing there. He had dressed up for the occasion, wearing a tailored black suit and a bright red tie. He looked devastatingly handsome as he brushed back his bangs from his eyes.

"What's the big idea? We're not going out to-night," Ryan said, slapping him on the back as he passed by to drop the keys on the desk.

Dan looked over at Jenny with an enticing half-smile. "I wanted to impress the lady." His intense stare melted her heart.

Ryan turned to Jenny. "Are you impressed?" She blushed in response, saying nothing.

Dan chuckled at her reaction. "I'd say that's a definite yes."

Shrugging his shoulders, Ryan muttered, "I would never think to get all dressed up when all we're going to do is take off our clothes."

Dan took Jenny's hand and planted a tender kiss on it. Then he looked up at Ryan. "You still have a lot to learn, grasshopper."

Jenny's heart raced being near him again. When he turned on slow music and took her in his arms to dance, she about swooned. "You look good tonight," she purred as he pressed his hand against the small of her back.

"And you look ravishing," he told her. Jenny looked up into his dark brown eyes and found herself utterly entranced by them.

Ryan cut in and took her from Dan's arms. "Two can play at that game." He twirled her and then bent her over in a dramatic fashion before kissing her on the lips. Jenny giggled when he brought her back up. "Where did that come from, Rye?"

"I saw it in a movie once. How was it?"

"It was... romantic." Ryan kissed her again and twirled her around the room a couple of more times before guiding her to the bed. She looked up at the two of them with her long dark hair splayed out on the bedspread.

"Yep, totally ravishing," Dan repeated. He leaned over her and brushed his lips against hers. The light kiss drove her wild. He knew how to play her body like a well-oiled instrument.

Jenny glanced over and saw Ryan ripping his clothes off. He stopped in midstream. "Oh yeah, I forgot. I'm just anxious to get started." Rye was so cute these days. The normally serious and controlled businessman now reminded her of an overeager teenager. He disappeared into the bathroom, asking Dan, "Did you bring what I asked?"

"Yep, it's on the counter in there. I got a brand new one just for you, because I know how you are."

Ryan's warm laughter echoed in the bathroom. "Good thinking. That would have bugged me to distraction."

She looked at Dan questioningly, but he only smiled. "Ryan has been looking forward to this for days. I'm not spoiling the surprise." He pulled her up off the bed and began leisurely undressing her. Once he had her down to her lingerie, she turned the tables and started undoing his tie. She pulled the material from his collar and let it fall to the floor. Then she slowly undid each button.

Dan looked down at her and growled under his breath. His erection strained against his black dress pants. Jenny rubbed it teasingly.

"You little vixen," he complained huskily.

Ryan came out of the bathroom with a tube of lubricant and his cock covered in it. Jenny did a quick double-take. "Are you serious?" she asked, completely shocked that he wanted to take her anally. It was the last thing she would have expected from Ryan.

He shrugged his shoulders and said with a boyish grin. "What can I say? It looked too fun to pass up."

Dan removed the last of her clothing and helped

her onto the bed. Jenny felt tingly all over. She couldn't believe Rye wanted to share this with her. Dan instructed him, "Now, you have to let her take the lead. It is going to feel fucking fantastic and you'll want to slam it in deep, but resist the urge. Let Jenny tell you when she is ready."

Ryan nodded his head, looking at her lustfully.

She was already on all fours, excited to try this new venture with Ryan. He moved into position behind her and immediately pushed his cock against her tight sphincter. Jenny squealed in surprise and scooted away from him.

"Slow down, man! You have to lube your partner first. You'll need to make Jenny all slippery both inside and out for it to feel good. Be gentle with her, for God's sake."

Ryan sighed in frustration. "Sorry, Jen. It's just that I'm feeling extra horny right now."

Jenny felt a twinge of fear when Ryan squeezed the gel between her buttocks. Dan was the only one she'd had this way and he was an experienced lover. Rye, on the other hand, was an overenthusiastic novice.

She bit her lip when his index finger pushed into her tight hole, breaking through her body's initial resistance. Dan told him, "You want to completely coat the inside and help her muscles to relax at the same time."

Ryan pushed his finger in deeper and her muscles tightened around it. "Damn, you're tight, Jen." He started gently thrusting his finger in and out of her ass while Dan massaged her back and shoulders. She moaned in pleasure, enjoying the multiple sensations. When her body relaxed enough, she announced, "I'm ready for you, Rye." He pulled his finger out and replaced it with the warm head of his cock.

"Remember, let her take the lead," Dan repeated.

Jenny started rocking back on Ryan's hard shaft. His was thin and straight as an arrow. She wondered if he would feel different. Dan reached between her legs and started stimulating her clit. Her juices began flowing and her body opened up for Ryan. The head of his cock slid in and both of them cried out in unison.

"Don't move," Dan commanded.

Ryan remained still as Jenny's body adjusted to the infiltration. When she felt her muscles relax again, she started pushing Ryan in deeper. He grabbed onto her hips, but Dan barked, "Let her lead, don't you dare take over yet." Jenny had to smile. The dynamic between the two men was amusing.

Dan continued to flick across her clit with his fingers while Ryan advanced ever deeper into her ass. "Oh God, Jen, this feels amazing," he groaned.

She loved that he was taking pleasure in her body, so Jenny started thrusting against his cock in an attempt to encompass his entire length. "Oh fuck!" he cried. "Fuck it to hell, that feels good!"

Jenny stifled a grin. She looked over at Dan. He

leaned down and kissed her as he rubbed her clit with fervor. "Come for him, Jenny."

His low voice sent a shiver down her spine that traveled straight to her groin. When his tongue parted her lips, she moaned in pleasure. Jenny concentrated on Ryan's cock filling her up as Dan stoked an unquenchable fire between her legs. In truth, she didn't want it to stop but the telltale signs of her impending orgasm were upon her.

"Yes, baby," whispered Dan. "Give into it." She started moaning louder. "Tell him what's happening."

She kissed him again before purring to Ryan, "I'm about to come."

"Do it, Jen. Let me feel it," Ryan encouraged.

Dan locked lips with her as the fire took over. His fingers were relentless when the orgasm claimed her. Ryan failed to follow Dan's rule and thrust his cock deep into her ass, but it was exactly what she needed and she whimpered in complete rapture. The peak of the climax seemed to go on forever before it finally ebbed away.

Ryan bent down and whispered, "Was it good, Jen?" She nodded, unable to speak. "Can I start thrusting now? I have a serious case of blue balls."

Dan scoffed, "Seriously, Ryan, you just started fucking the woman. I doubt you have blue balls."

"I've been fantasizing about this for days. I *need* release."

Jenny felt much looser after her intense climax and was willing to take his manly thrusts. "Be gentle,

Rye. Your cock is so big," she murmured. Jenny could just imagine the grin on his face. It was fun stroking his ego, although she was partially serious.

Needing no further encouragement, Ryan pulled out and then pushed back into her slowly, going as deep as her body could take. The length of him took Jenny's breath away. She closed her eyes and concentrated on relaxing to take in more of him as Ryan's tempo increased. He began making grunting gasps, a sound that was new to her. "Oh fuck, this is going to be a big one," he warned before he seized her hips and gave one final thrust, shooting his seed deep within her.

"Jenny, Jenny…" he whispered afterwards, running his hands over her ass. "That was fucking amazing."

"Pull out slowly," Dan told him. "Her body will resist, so you'll hurt her if you don't."

Ryan thoughtfully disengaged and flopped down on the bed. He stared up at the ceiling with a look of sheer bliss on his face. "Best sex ever."

Jenny leaned over and kissed his hairless chest. "So glad I could please you."

Ryan lay there for several minutes in a state of ecstasy and then he suddenly stiffened. The old Ryan returned when he looked at his hands and cock as if he could see invisible germs. "I better clean up." He pushed off the bed and left them.

"He'll never change," Dan said.

"Yeah, but you seem to bring out a new side to Rye. I've never seen him get that excited before."

"It's all you, baby," Dan said, brushing her hair away from her sweaty face. "No man can resist such beauty."

She ran her fingers through his blond hair. "You're wrong. Ryan has never been like this with me."

"It's only because he didn't understand what he had," Dan murmured, nuzzling her neck. He began caressing her breasts and pinching her nipples lightly, making her body ache with need of him.

Ryan came out of the bathroom and announced, "Jen, I think it's time."

"Time for what?"

Dan growled into her neck, saying nothing. She looked back at Ryan questioningly, but he just grinned at her.

Love Expressed

It was obvious she was the *only* one who didn't know what was about to happen and it irritated her. "Don't leave me in the dark, Rye. I need to know what's going on."

"Dan and I talked."

"You seem to do an awful lot of that without me," she grumbled.

Ryan sat down next to her on the bed. "There are some things the two of us have to work out. Surely you can understand that." Jenny blushed; she could only imagine what their conversations were like. How did two men decide the logistics of sharing one woman? "Anyway, I've come to accept that the two of you love each other. Because of that, I am willing to let him engage you by traditional means."

Dan spoke up. "He has agreed to let me make love to you, Jenny."

She looked at Dan and saw the sparkle in his

eye. *So that's why he dressed up this evening.* They were going to make love for the first time. The prospect set her heart racing. He took her hand in his. "Are you ready for me to love you properly?"

She nodded her head, her poor heart threatening to burst. He leaned over and kissed her before moving down between her legs. He stroked the outside of her pussy first, exploring it with his fingers and then followed it up with licks from his talented tongue.

Ryan moved to her breasts and began caressing and squeezing them. He took a nipple into his mouth and sucked on it lavishly. "I can never get enough of these beauties," he whispered.

Jenny closed her eyes to drink in the love from both men. Could there be anything better than having two men whose only mission was to love and please her?

She felt Dan's fingers explore her opening. They soon found their way inside. He easily located her G-spot and began stroking it lightly, teasing her with his touch. When he had her moaning in delight, his fingers retreated and he got in position to take her.

He pressed his cock against her moist entrance. She looked into his eyes and forgot to breathe. Dan prolonged their first time by entering her slowly with just the head of his thick cock. She was barely aware of Ryan playing with her nipples as Dan pulled back out and then reentered her, taking his time to push the entire length of his manhood inside her velvety depths. It felt even better than she imagined.

Her chest started pounding and she gasped for air. She'd forgotten to breathe again. Ryan looked up from her breasts. "You okay?"

She nodded and then looked at Dan.

His eyes never left her. He slowly pulled all the way out and reentered. It felt even better the second time. The sensations Dan was able to create with his magic fingers dancing over her body, he now created with his shaft. He caressed and loved her with his manhood, bringing her to the edge and then backing away. Building up the intensity, but not allowing the release.

"Can I kiss her?" Dan asked hoarsely.

Ryan moved away and Dan leaned over her, kissing her deeply as he rolled his hips rhythmically, pushing his cock into her. It was powerfully sexy. When he pulled away, he continued to look at her. Ryan returned to her breasts, pleasuring them with sheer adoration.

Dan took his time, savoring her and teasing her with his sensual penetration. Jenny never wanted the session to end. She played with Ryan's curly brown hair while Dan loved her with his manhood. It was perfect, nothing could compare.

He finally gave into the pleasure and started rubbing the head of his cock against her G-spot with short quick thrusts. "No, Dan, stop. Stop," she begged.

"I want you to come."

"Not yet…"

Dan wasn't taking no for an answer. He continued thrusting into her at just the right angle until the feelings became impossible to control. She let go and cried out as her muscles contracted forcefully around his considerable girth. Ryan kissed her, wanting to be a part of their lovemaking. Jenny wrapped her arms around him as she continued to come around Dan's cock. She felt him suddenly change angles as he pushed further into her.

He commanded hoarsely, "Feel my orgasm, Jenny."

She closed her eyes and felt Dan's shaft pulsate rhythmically as he released his essence. It was the most erotic thing she had experienced yet—this feeling of their juices mingling together. She darted her tongue into Ryan's mouth and licked across the roof of it. His passionate groan caused her pussy to contract pleasurably around Dan's shaft one final time.

Once again, the three found themselves lying on the bed together staring at the ceiling with Jenny in the middle and a guy on either side.

"I could get used to this," Dan stated.

"Me too…" Jenny sighed contentedly.

"Actually," Ryan said, propping his head up with one hand, "I've been thinking about that. Dan, how would you feel about joining us at the apartment? Until you find a suitable apartment of your own, of course. We only have the one bedroom, but we have a sleeper sofa in the living room and we could always turn the office into another bedroom if you want."

Jenny stared at Ryan in shock. Was he seriously proposing they make this threesome a legitimate ménage à trois? The thought both thrilled and scared her. Would they be able to maintain this dynamic or would they end up ruining the beautiful thing they'd just created?

"Don't feel you have to, man. My coworker is willing to put up with me a while longer."

"It's not just for you, Dan. Jenny and I would enjoy having you around. Wouldn't you, Boo?"

She looked from Ryan to Dan and back to Ryan again. "It seems crazy to me."

"People have made it work before. No reason we can't try. If it works, it works. If not, c'est la vie," he said, shrugging his shoulders.

Jenny stared at the ceiling again. Was she really being given the chance to enjoy both men on a daily basis? *What would the neighbors say?* A smile crept across her face. *Who cares...* Jenny had only one real concern. "I don't want anyone to get hurt."

"I think if we keep the lines of communication open it shouldn't be a problem," Dan told her. "I'm game if you are."

Jenny grinned. "A real ménage à trois, huh? Hmm... just so you know, Dan, Ryan and I share in all the chores. We have an equal partnership in everything."

"In everything," Ryan murmured, nibbling her ear.

"You forget that I lived with Kelly for years. I'm

used to doing all the work. It shouldn't be a problem." Dan circled her left breast with his index finger.

Are we really going to do this?

Apparently so… Ryan and Jenny helped Dan move his stuff into their apartment the next day. They started the process of converting the office into a second bedroom, feeling that Dan needed privacy just as much as they did.

Jenny knew bringing a third person into the relationship would mean a lot of adjustment on everyone's part. She hoped they could survive the initial change. Her greatest fear, however, was that Ryan and Dan would grow jealous of each other as time passed.

On their first night as a threesome, after a meal of garlic chicken—a joke on Jenny's part—the three sat on the couch watching the evening news. Ryan turned towards Dan and said nonchalantly, "I'd really like to know where Jenny's G-spot is."

"What? You haven't tried to find it yet?"

Ryan cleared his throat. "Actually, we did try… a couple of times."

"Oh, well, I can show you right now if you'd like."

Jenny looked at them both in mock disgust. "I'm not an object you can just grope when you feel like it." Her pussy was already wet, but she wasn't about to tell them that.

"I was going to ask your permission before I demonstrated," Dan assured her.

"It's really in your best interest for me to learn. I want to rock your world, Boo."

She winked at Rye and playfully complained, "I suppose…" Jenny slipped off her shorts and then peeled off her panties. It seemed surreal to be watching the national news while her men played with her eager little body. *A taste of heaven.*

Not one to rush things, Dan fingered and teased the outside of her pussy while he explained. "It will be about three inches in. You should be able to reach it with your middle finger. It's on the roof of her vagina and feels like a round lump."

"Well, that sounds sexy," she complained.

"Just telling it like it is." Dan chuckled lightly. "Her G-spot will get harder as you stimulate it. You want to curl your finger to rub it just right." He demonstrated the motion for Ryan. "You'll know you've hit it if you observe her reaction."

Dan slowly inserted his finger while Ryan watched. Jenny felt like a science experiment, but she found it kinky and exciting. He felt around for a second. She twitched when he rubbed against it. "Ah, did you see that?" He stroked her just right and the fire began building deep inside. She shifted, breathing heavy. Dan pulled his finger out and looked at Ryan. "You give it a try."

Ryan stared at her dark mound and then gave

her a quick peck on the cheek before pushing his middle finger into her hot depths. Jenny spread her legs further and shifted to help him. He brushed against it once and she jumped, but then his finger moved away.

"Did you notice when you hit it?" Dan asked.

"What, I did?"

"You have to watch her, man. A woman prefers it when you can read her rather than making her tell you what to do."

Ryan sighed in frustration. She could tell he was nervous about failing in front of Dan. Jenny encouraged him, "You found it, Rye. I'll try to let you know this time."

"No. I want to learn to read you," he said earnestly. How sweet was that? Jenny bit her lip as Ryan explored her with his finger. Once again, he hit the sensitive spot and she shuddered. He looked at her and said confidently, "Found it." She nodded with a pleased smile. Ryan began rubbing it and although the heat started, it was not nearly as pleasurable as when Dan did it.

Dan was watching her intently, and explained. "If she isn't getting wetter, you need to stroke her differently. I like to mimic the feel as if I am thrusting my cock nice and deep but not too fast."

Ryan changed the rhythm of his stroke and she felt an immediate difference. She moaned softly. He leaned over and kissed her, losing the spot. She saw a look of panic on his face, but he quickly found his way back and soon had her pussy singing again.

"Just keep it steady and she'll be coming in no time."

"Oh Rye, it really feels good," she purred.

He smiled slightly, but didn't lose his look of concentration. Soon her heart was pounding and her groin muscles contracted. She grabbed onto the couch for support as her hips pushed against his hand. Jenny cried out loudly, wanting Ryan to know how much he was pleasing her, but became silent when the massive orgasm hit. Wave after intense wave rolled over her.

"Shit, I can feel her coming around my finger," he said in awe. Warm liquid gushed as it ended.

"Oh yeah, that was a strong one," Dan commented.

Ryan couldn't hide his feeling of pride. "I did good, didn't I, Jenny Boo?" He pressed his lips against hers. "You've never come like that for me before."

"It was amazing, Rye. Oh, my God, it was amazing! Thank you." She looked down at his crotch and then Dan's, noticing they both were horny. The power to make two men lust after her at the same time was exhilarating. "Why don't we retire to the bedroom so I can thank you both?"

Dan's eyes lit up at the suggestion, but Jenny wondered if Ryan would mind doing it on their bed. Up until then, it had been his territory only. The lust in his eyes made it quite clear that sex was more important than sentimentality. Dan had her naked in no time, but Ryan was already undressed. He laid her on the bed, leaving Dan to undress himself quickly or be left behind.

"I want to fuck my girlfriend's pussy right now," Ryan declared.

"Then I'm going to enjoy my girlfriend's mouth," Dan replied.

They both called her *girlfriend*. Jenny loved it.

The men moved into position. Ryan lifted her legs up and plowed right in. Evidently, seeing her come was a major turn-on for him. Jenny laid her head back over the edge of the bed for Dan. He moved next to her and she guided his shaft in. She swirled her tongue around his cock and then started sucking hard. Her body was humming with excitement. Instead of lasting for hours, Ryan came in ten minutes pounding her heartily non-stop.

Jenny was still teasing Dan's cock when Ryan pulled out. He lay back and watched her pleasure Dan. She suddenly got a wild hair and pushed his cock to the back of her throat, swallowing hard. His shaft traveled further in.

Dan groaned loudly, obviously taken by surprise. She grabbed his buttocks and pushed his cock in even deeper, feeling it slide down her throat. When she couldn't take anymore, she pulled him out.

"What the fuck was that?" Ryan asked, sitting up.

"Jenny is learning how to deepthroat," Dan growled huskily.

She turned her head and smiled at Ryan. "It was

something I picked up at the cabin."

"Why didn't you tell me?"

"I thought it would gross you out."

Ryan shook his head. "There's nothing gross about that."

Jenny looked up at Dan hungrily. "I want to try again."

He traced the line of her delicate neck. "Any time, woman. You know I love the feel of it."

She pulled him into her after taking a deep breath. She swallowed and felt the head of his cock travel back down her throat. This time when she couldn't take him any deeper, she pulled him partially out and then back in. He cried out and she felt his shaft start pulsating. She couldn't believe she'd made him come so easily. Jenny had to pull his shaft out before he was finished coming, so she let the rest of his tangy essence cover her tongue. Dan was shaking like a leaf when he moved away from her.

"I literally saw your cock travel down her throat," Ryan said in astonishment.

"I know," Dan grunted. "It's part of the reason I like it so much. It's visually stimulating and when you add the control of her throat... it's too much." Dan bent down and kissed Jenny all over her face and neck. "Oh my God, you continue to amaze me, woman!"

Although Jenny felt a little sore from the at-tempt, she was very happy she'd tried it. Making Dan quiver made her feel like the sexiest woman alive.

The three ended up falling asleep in the bed together. Dan woke up the next morning and showered, while the other two contemplated getting up. "Morning, Boo," Ryan said, kissing her on the forehead.

She grazed his lips lightly with her fingertip. "Morning."

"I don't think I have ever felt this alive before. I feel like a million bucks." He jumped out of the bed and flexed his muscles as he smiled down at her.

"You look it, Rye."

"Jen, I think we've stumbled onto something amazing here. I can't wait to come home and play together tonight."

After he left the room, Jenny realized that her feelings for Ryan were changing. Not that long ago she would have said she loved him but was not *in love* with him. But now… things were definitely different.

Jenny rolled out of bed and started her morning routine. She saw both of her men off, giving each a kiss before they drove to their respective jobs. Jenny jumped in her own car, but just as she was shutting the door, she heard a female scream hysterically. It was followed by the angry squeal of tires.

Before she could turn to see what was going on, the vehicle was gone. She convinced herself the woman was just having a bad start to her Monday. *It's not Kelly…*

She spent her lunch googling "threesomes". She

was curious what other people were doing to make it work and was surprised to find a lot of information on the subject. There were chat rooms, blogs, and even websites focused on the benefits and pitfalls of living a real-life ménage à trois.

Apparently, its official name was polyamory. Jenny even found a website devoted to helping threesomes find each other. *Who knew?*

Three people who loved each other and lived under the same roof were rare, but not unheard of. Their little bit of nirvana was possible if the three of them put a lot of time and love into making it work. Jenny was still worried that her two men would grow jealous of one another but for now, things seemed perfect. Ryan was enjoying his newfound sexual appetite and Dan was in her arms again.

Being in love with two men was truly a fairytale come true, but Jenny couldn't shake the feeling that fairytales weren't meant to last.

Blissfully Broken

L ast night had marked Jenny's first evening living with two men—an official ménage à trois. The night had been an adventure of firsts that made Jenny's loins quiver even now at her work desk. She gazed out of her office window to the mountain range in the distance, marveling how those mountains and one timely blizzard had changed everything.

The scandalous knowledge that she would soon be going home to the adoration of two passionate men was almost more than she could handle, but handle it she would—dreams were made of this.

Dan called her near the end of the day. "How's work going, baby?"

"Best Monday ever! And you?"

"Have to say knowing I'm coming home to you has made the day a thousand times better."

"I agree. I can't wait to kiss you all over when I see you."

"Don't start or I won't be able to leave my desk without embarrassing myself."

She purred seductively into the phone, "Now I *am* tempted to tease you."

He cleared his throat loudly and paused for a second. "So… how did Ryan seem this morning?"

She grinned to herself and let him change the subject. "The same as us, excited about this new arrangement."

"I have to admit when he first proposed a ménage I didn't think it would work. I assumed he'd be too jealous to let me touch you, but that hasn't been the case at all."

"No, it's like I'm getting to know Ryan on a completely different level. I never thought he had a wild side to him and I've been with him for years."

"Yeah, surprising how the combination of the three of us seems to work well."

Jenny *almost* told Dan about the strange scene at the apartment earlier that morning. She'd heard a girl scream, followed by the angry squeal of tires, and she was worried that it might have been Kelly. After thinking about it all day long, however, she had chalked it up to her own paranoia and guilt.

Ryan called just as she was turning off her office lights. "Hey, Jen. Can't wait to get home to you."

She smiled into the phone. "Me too, Rye."

"Have you talked to Dan today?"

Jen giggled. "He just called a few minutes ago. I think he wanted to see how you were doing."

"What did you tell him?"

"That we all seem to be on the same page."

Ryan sounded relieved. "So he's okay with it?"

"More than okay. He is anxious to join us at home."

"Good. Then I'll see you in a few, Boo. Drive safely."

"Will do. You do the same." She hung up the phone and turned off the lights before starting the twenty-minute drive to their apartment. She looked in her rearview mirror and swore Kelly's red Camaro was behind her. Soon the car was riding on her ass. She slammed on her brakes to force Kelly to pull back, but she kept right on her tail. *What the hell, Kelly?*

Her ex-best friend must have suspected the three of them were living together now. It made sense that Kelly was pissed. Jenny would be too if the tables were turned, but that didn't excuse her for driving like a fucking lunatic. She felt the first shiver of fear when Kelly hit the back of her car. Although it was only a tap, it proved that the woman was truly mental.

Jenny sped up to avoid another collision and almost crashed into the car in front when the vehicle slowed down for a right turn. She quickly glanced in the rearview mirror and saw that Kelly had disappeared. In her place was a cop's flashing lights. Jenny groaned and pulled off to the side of the road.

"Miss, would you like to explain what you were doing?"

Jenny looked up and saw the same officer who had stopped her once before. She started shaking, the endorphins kicking in too late to do her any good.

"You again!" he barked.

Jenny bowed her head. *Can this get any worse?* She begged her hands to stop trembling, but they shook even worse and the officer noticed.

"Get out of the car, now!"

He made her walk a straight line on the shoulder of the road and then touch her nose with her eyes closed. Although she easily found her nose, her hands continued to shake uncontrollably.

"What's wrong with you? Are you on drugs?" he accused, shining a small light in her eyes.

"No, I was being chased by my ex-girlfriend. She hit the back of my car." Jenny pointed frantically to her bumper.

"Girlfriend, huh?" he said condescendingly.

"My friend who is a girl," Jenny stammered, not wanting him to get the wrong idea.

The cop shook his head in disgust. He strode to the back of the car and looked the bumper over. "There are a few scratches here, but no real damage. Nothing to indicate you were hit." He stared at her disapprovingly. "I did not see anyone chasing you. However, I did witness your speeding car swerve severely to avoid a turning vehicle. You do not appear to be safe to drive, so I am taking you in."

Jenny sobbed as he helped her into the cop car. It smelled of sweat, tobacco and humiliation.

Dan and Ryan arrived at the police station together a half-hour after she called. She didn't give them any details, just that she wanted to go home.

The two men burst into the police station and ran to her. They hugged and kissed Jenny, forgetting there was a roomful of police. The officer watched the three in disapproval. "Disgusting," he snarled. "Our paths better not cross again, miss. If they do, I will make it my personal mission to revoke your license."

He thrust the paperwork in her face and walked off. Dan pulled her into his arms. "It was Kelly, wasn't it?"

She looked up at him in surprise. "How did you know?"

"I told you she is bad news. I'm so sorry, baby. So, so sorry." He kissed her again, squeezing her so tight it restricted her breathing.

Ryan was visibly upset. "What the hell are you two talking about?"

Jenny squelched her guilt about not telling him. "I tried to talk to Kelly a few days ago and apparently I really pissed her off."

Dan let go of her so he could talk directly to Ryan. "Kelly called me and bawled me out because Jenny went to her work. Kelly said some pretty malicious things, but I trusted once she calmed down it would be okay." He glanced over at Jenny. "I also instructed Jenny not to contact her again. I always suspected Kelly was certifiable, but she proved it tonight."

"The cop doesn't believe me," Jenny cried. "He claims he didn't see anything."

Ryan took charge of the situation. "You are going to file a complaint. Whether or not he saw it, we need to have the incident on record." He lifted her chin up and looked into her red-rimmed eyes. "We won't let anything happen to you, Jen."

Dan asked Ryan, "Do you think she knows about the three of us?"

Jenny admitted to both of them, "I think she was at our apartment this morning and saw me kiss both of you."

Dan's look of concern contorted into a frown. "Why didn't you tell me?"

"Well, I wasn't sure."

Ryan wrapped his arms around her. "From now on you have to tell me *everything*." He looked over Jenny's head and added to Dan, "That goes for you, too."

That night the three ate their meal in silence. Worry flowed tangibly from both men, making Jenny antsy. She got the distinct impression their ménage was in jeopardy.

Dan confirmed it when he stated, "I think it is best if I go."

"No, Dan!" she protested. "You can't let Kelly win."

"Maybe Dan is right," Ryan replied. "If she is mental, we don't want to do anything to set her off."

"I refuse to live my life in fear!" She looked at

Dan in disbelief. "Do you really want to give her that power over us?"

He cupped her chin tenderly. "No, but I don't want you to get hurt either."

Jenny gazed into his dark brown eyes and pleaded, "You'll hurt me if you leave."

He groaned and glanced over at Ryan. "What do you think?"

She was sure he would choose the safest path, but he surprised her. "If anything more happens we are slapping a restraining order on Kelly."

Jenny jumped up and gave Ryan a hug. She leaned over and whispered in his ear, "Thanks, Rye," before kissing him on the lips.

Jenny was determined to draw them closer as a threesome, so she used a Dan tactic. "Have either of you ever wanted to try a little DP?"

Dan instantly locked eyes with her and a mischievous grin played at the corners of his lips.

"What's DP?" Ryan asked.

Jenny blushed a hot shade of pink when she explained. "You know, double penetration. Two guys at the same time…"

He looked at her in shock. "You really want to try that?"

She smiled nervously. "I don't know… it might be fun."

"Yet again, you astound me," Dan said with conviction. He leaned over and gave her a passionate kiss.

"Have you done that with a girl before?" Ryan

asked him.

"Nope, only in my dreams," Dan said, staring at Jenny hungrily.

She wondered with a smile, *How long has he been fantasizing about taking me that way?*

However, Ryan was concerned for her. "Don't you think it'll hurt, Jen?"

Her heart started racing when she thought about it. "I don't know if it will hurt, but I want to try."

"If it does, we stop. Simple as that," Dan answered.

Ryan growled in Jenny's ear, "I'm claiming your pussy if we are really doing this."

Dan overheard him and joked. "I think Jenny wouldn't have it any other way, blue balls."

Jenny giggled, remembering how overeager Ryan had been when he took her anally the first time. She bit her lip in excitement. "So we're agreed then?"

Dan got up and walked to the kitchen. He came back with a bottle of wine and three glasses. "I think you need to get *real* relaxed first. I'll get the massaging oil ready. Ryan, you get some candles lit in the bedroom." He poured her a full glass, handing it to her with a look of adoration. "You are by far the sexiest woman I've ever known."

Jenny sipped the wine while her men got their bedroom ready. Her pussy was already humming at the mere thought of taking both of them at the same time. When Ryan and Dan returned to her, she poured them both a glass. The three drank leisurely, letting the idea of what they were about to do sink in.

Dan gazed at her with a gleam in his eye. "So... what made you want to try this?"

"I love you both and I was thinking today how much I want to make love to you at the same time. To *show* you in action how I feel."

Ryan shifted in his seat and cleared his throat. "I can't say I have ever entertained the idea before, but now that you've mentioned it I can't think of anything else."

She leaned over and glanced at his crotch. Oh yeah, Rye was thinking a *lot* about it.

A Little DP

Jenny kissed Ryan on the lips and purred, "I'm glad you are open to trying something different like this."

"You have me doing things I never imagined, but I've loved every damn thing," he said, returning her kiss.

Dan played with a strand of her hair. "I can't believe you're real, Jenny. You *must* be a figment of my imagination." He caressed her cheek lightly before grasping her neck and pressing his mouth to hers. His tongue danced over her lips. She opened herself to him, moaning softly when his tongue darted into her mouth and tasted her.

Ryan cupped her breasts while Dan continued to kiss her. Her nipples were already hard and responded eagerly when he lightly brushed over the material of her blouse. "So sexy," he murmured as one hand traveled down her stomach, making its way to her burning sex. She spread her legs to give him access, moaning into Dan's mouth when Ryan moved her panties to the side and caressed her swollen lips with his fingers. Their heavy petting continued for several minutes before his finger disappeared into her moist depths.

Dan was turned on by her soft moaning and thrust his tongue deeper into her mouth. She darted into his and they explored each other as Ryan's finger explored her inner walls. She twitched when he found her G-spot.

Ryan's lips came down on her neck and he began biting and sucking lightly as he caressed her secret spot. She panted and squirmed in response. Both men slipped their hands under her shirt and played with her nipples. *Nirvana!*

She tried to break the kiss with Dan to gain some control, but he held her chin, allowing no escape. Her pelvic muscles tensed as a hard contraction milked Ryan's finger. He groaned into her neck when he felt her orgasm begin.

Jenny gasped, the first wave taking her by surprise. Dan teased her with his tongue as Ryan sucked on her neck, causing a biting pain. It added to the overall experience and her pussy creamed his finger in a powerful orgasm. She whimpered into Dan's mouth as it overtook her.

"I love it when I feel you come," Ryan whispered hoarsely. This from the man who used to accept fake orgasms without question. Oh, how she loved him!

Both men disengaged and Dan handed over her

wine glass with a wink. "Have another drink before we take you to our little love nest."

She purred, her whole body relaxed after her climax. It made her confident she could take them both. She downed the wine quickly, not wanting to lose her momentum.

Ryan held out his hand to her. She took it and let him lead her into the bedroom with Dan following close behind. The room had been transformed into a romantic paradise with lit candles, soft music and peppermint incense.

"Nice," Jenny complimented.

Ryan started unbuttoning her top. His hands moved sensually as he undid each one. He nuzzled her neck and murmured sweet nothings as he undressed her. Again, she was amazed at the incredible lover he'd become.

Once her breasts were exposed to the air, Dan knelt down and freed her from her skirt and panties. Both men caressed every inch of her skin with their fingers. She laid her head back on Ryan's shoulder and succumbed to their dual attention.

She groaned loudly when Dan licked the length of her sex and then started flicking his tongue against her erect clit. "You're so tasty after you come," he muttered between licks. His thumb slipped inside her pussy while his index finger caressed her puckered hole.

Jenny's knees buckled and Ryan had to catch her. "I think we should move this to the bed," he stated.

Both men stripped before they made their way to the large bed. Dan's defined chest with blond curls begged to be caressed. She snuck a quick peek at his thick cock and wondered how it would feel this time. He noticed her stare and smiled as he brushed back his long bangs. The simple gesture melted Jenny's heart—it always had.

Ryan lay on the bed first so she turned her attention on him. His chest was smooth and his shaft already rigid, eager for the festivities to begin. He stroked his long cock slowly with one hand, commanding lustfully, "Come and make love to me, beautiful."

She gazed into his jade eyes as she crawled to him. He helped her straddle his hips and then groaned in pleasure as she eased his lengthy, thin shaft into her moist depths. Having just come, her body easily enveloped his entire length. She leaned over and kissed him, trying to express with her body the deep love she felt for the man.

Meanwhile, Dan thoroughly lubricated his thick member before getting onto the bed to join them. "Baby, I'm going to take this *real* slow. Normally you are the one in control, but it's not possible with DP. You need to trust that I'll be gentle."

She looked back towards him and purred, "I trust you completely, Dan."

He caressed her buttocks with reverence. "You're so incredibly beautiful, Jenny. Your copper Cherokee skin is such a turn-on." He pulled her long black hair back and stroked it lovingly with one hand while the other began playing with her ass. He ran his index finger around the rim, covering it in lubricant and then he barely pushed against it before retreating. He teased her little hole, making it crave deeper penetration.

She started grinding against Ryan's cock, rocking on it so that the movement pushed Dan's finger deeper into her ass. She felt the difference immediately. With a shaft inside her, his finger seemed so much bigger but his touch remained sensual and tender. Dan took his time and soon had her moaning in pleasure.

She felt him slip another finger inside her taut hole. She groaned as her muscles constricted around it, but her body began to relax and accepted his gentle stroking. He withdrew his fingers and moved into position. Jenny tensed when she felt him spread her apart and press the head of his cock against her anus.

"Relax, baby. We've got all the time in the world." His magic hands started massaging her back as he pushed a little harder. Her body resisted, but he did not force it. He kept the constant pressure as he caressed her back and played with her hair. She felt her body slowly open to him and the head of his cock slipped in. She gasped at the feeling of incredible fullness it gave her.

Ryan grunted underneath her. "Oh shit…" He started to thrust, but Dan stopped him.

"Don't move yet. Wait until I'm in all the way." His hands continued their magic as his cock slowly inched its way into her exceedingly tight ass. She gasped a couple of times and had to remind her body to allow the invasion. There came a point when it felt like she was going to burst with their two dicks lodged so deep inside her.

"Kiss her, Ryan," Dan commanded.

Ryan pressed his mouth against hers, loving her with his lips. She became lost in the kiss and Dan was able to finally push his full length into her. The three lay there in silence, reveling in the connection.

Dan braced himself to begin thrusting. He told Ryan, "When I pull out you'll want to push in. Let's start off slow and see how Jenny likes it."

Ryan grabbed her hips and the two began thrusting. It was uncomfortable at first as they struggled to find a rhythm. She stifled her cries, not wanting them to stop. When they found their stride, their cocks completely filled her like nothing she'd ever experienced. Her body started to tingle and ache pleasantly as it surrendered to their lovemaking.

She closed her eyes and concentrated on the extraordinary feeling of taking the cocks of both lovers at once. She was completely at their mercy, unable to move as they made love to her body. "Are you okay, baby?" Dan asked.

"Yes," she breathed softly.

Ryan groaned in pleasure. "You look so sexy with my love mark." He grazed her neck with his fingertips. "God, I love you, Boo…"

She smiled down at him, excited that she could

please him this way. "I love you, Rye." He kissed her again, stopping the motion for a second.

Dan waited patiently until Ryan broke the embrace. Then Dan flipped her hair to one side and said, "Give me a kiss, too." She turned her head and he leaned forward, forcing his dick further into her ass. Dan darted his tongue into her mouth as his fingers played with one of her nipples. "I love you, woman."

She groaned, excited by the intimacy of this unique encounter. Loving both men at the same time was... out of this world.

The two started up again. She could feel the combination of their cocks pressing hard against her G-spot with each thrust. "Faster," she panted. They increased their pace and her body responded immediately. Her toes curled as a tingling chill took over. Jenny started moaning, but moaning wasn't enough. Soon she was screaming, totally caught up in the intensity of their dual thrusting.

Ryan cried out, "Fuck, I can't stop it!" His body tensed under her and then his cock pushed deep inside, pulsing with each release of his seed.

Dan kept up with his thrusting, murmuring hoarsely, "Give into it, Jenny. Let yourself go." He concentrated his movements where he knew it would have the most effect.

She threw her head back and let out a lusty scream as her own climax hit. Dan grabbed onto her shoulders and rammed his cock in deeper as he orgasmed with her.

"Mark me," she growled passionately.

Dan's lips landed on the other side of her neck. He sucked hard as their climax peaked. Ryan fondled her breasts, tugging on her nipples to increase her pleasure. She milked his semi-hard cock with her intense orgasm and all three cried out as it ended.

She collapsed on Ryan's chest as Dan slowly pulled away from her. It took several minutes before she came back down to earth. "I love you both!" she finally gasped out.

"That was unreal, Jen," Ryan sighed.

Dan stroked her hair and gazed lovingly into her eyes. "Most beautiful woman in the world."

The three remained on the bed and fell asleep together. As Jenny drifted off, she smiled to herself. She'd successfully thwarted Kelly's attempt to break them up. Now they were connected on a level no one could penetrate.

But the Cracks Begin

Three months into their new arrangement, Jenny started noticing a change in Ryan. He was staying at work long after business hours and often came home agitated. The drive to succeed was slowly taking over his life again and Workaholic Ryan was not as nearly as fun as Threesome Ryan.

The three had agreed not to have intercourse unless all were present. It was fine with Jenny, because Dan spent that time cuddling with her or rubbing her feet. However, Ryan abruptly changed those dynamics one night after a particularly hard week at work.

He walked into the apartment looking completely beat and defeated. Ryan glanced over at Jenny on the couch in Dan's arms and barked, "Join me in the bedroom, Jen."

She gave Dan a questioning look, but followed behind Ryan. He shut the door and then collapsed on the bed. She cuddled up beside him and caressed his furrowed brow. "What's wrong, Rye?"

"I can't stand working late at night, knowing the two of you are together doing God knows what."

She stopped her gentle caress and looked at him in disbelief. "Nobody is doing anything behind your back, Ryan. We both care about you too much."

"Well... it's hard knowing he has all that time alone with you and I don't."

Jenny resumed stroking his forehead lovingly. "I'm here now."

Ryan leaned over and kissed her. He broke away and looked at her possessively. "I love you too much, Boo."

She smiled. "Not too much, just right." She snuggled up to him and kissed him again. The kiss quickly became serious when his tongue entered her mouth and played with hers. His hands started their own exploration, caressing her womanly curves and eventually making their way to her breasts. He began kneading them through her clothes. "I want you, Jen," he said raggedly.

"What about Dan?" she whispered.

"Just this one time. I've been through hell this week and all I want is to make love to my woman without thinking about anyone else."

She hesitated. As much as she wanted to comfort Ryan, it wasn't fair to Dan.

"Please," Ryan growled. "I *need* this."

She didn't resist when he began unbuttoning her shirt. He grunted when he realized he had her consent and ripped off her jeans next. He wasted no time taking off his clothes so that they both were naked on the bed except for her bra. He left that on, exclaiming, "I love red satin against your copper skin." He pulled down on the bra and exposed her nipple. Ryan took it into his mouth and sucked harder than usual. She cried out and he stopped.

"I apologize, I'm a little overeager tonight." He pulled down the material covering her other nipple and began his breast worship. He lost himself kissing, licking and sucking her luscious mounds of flesh. "I can never get enough of these," he murmured. *Always my breast man.*

Jenny heard Dan moving around in the kitchen and felt a twinge of guilt. "Maybe we shouldn't."

In response to her doubt, Ryan moved between her legs. He started licking her clit lightly, teasing her opening with his fingers. She relaxed under his ministrations and gave into the sexual tension he was creating. Her pussy started humming the more he played with her despite her reservations. He chuckled when a gush of wetness covered his fingers.

Ryan lay on top of her and pushed himself into her aching depths. "Do you feel that, Jen? Do you feel how hard you make me?" He started grunting loudly as he thrust into her. "You make me so crazy."

When his thrusts grew longer, she knew he was readying himself for an orgasm. He leaned over and kissed her neck, sucking hard as he came inside her. He left a love mark, one that Dan would not be able to miss. It worried her.

He rolled off, wrapping his hands around her and pulling her close. He started manually teasing her clit, knowing it wouldn't take long to get her off now that he was familiar with her body. "Come for me, Jen. Let me feel you come on my fingers again."

She tilted her head back into his chest, not really having a choice. Her body demanded release after such focused stimulation. She whimpered softly when the climax crested and her inner walls contracted around his fingers.

He groaned in satisfaction. "God, that feels incredible." After her body relaxed, he lay on his back and looked up at the ceiling. "I really needed this."

She looked at him with misgiving. "Rye, we'll have to talk to Dan."

His face contorted in anger and he snapped, "Fine! Can't believe I'm not allowed to spend time alone with my girlfriend in my own home." He pulled away from her and stomped off to the bathroom. She heard the shower turn on, so she started to dress.

Jenny didn't understand where the anger and jealousy were coming from. Dan was always respectful of Ryan and played by the rules they set without question.

She left the bedroom and found Dan cooking dinner. He took one look at her and put down the metal spoon he was stirring with. "What's going on?"

She shook her head slowly. "I don't know. Ryan

is acting weird today."

"Did you two just have sex?" he asked calmly.

Jenny felt the heat rise to her cheeks. "Yes."

"That's not good."

She looked at him with tears in her eyes. "I know." It was happening—their perfect threesome was starting to crumble after only a few months.

Ryan joined them several minutes later. He looked at the two of them without speaking and then sat down at the kitchen table. "What's for dinner?"

Dan nodded to Jenny. "Go ahead and sit. We'll talk while we eat." He put a large pot of chili in the middle of the table and handed out bowls. "Nothing fancy tonight."

Everyone served themselves in silence. Finally, Dan looked his best friend in the eye and asked, "What's up, Ryan?"

He didn't answer right away, chewing slowly on his food. "Look, it has been a rough week and I just needed some alone time with her. What's the big deal?" He added under his breath, "She was my girlfriend first, you know."

"I thought we agreed not to have sex as couples."

Ryan snorted. "Like you two haven't been doing it."

Dan's eyes narrowed. "We haven't, Ryan. I wouldn't go behind your back."

Ryan ignored the implied insult. "Well, like I said it's been rough at work lately. I needed to be with the woman I love."

"Do you want to change the rules then?" Dan pressed.

"No, not where you are concerned."

"What? So now you can make love to Jenny whenever you feel like it, but I can't?"

Jenny growled, "You two do realize I am in the room. The way I see it, all three of us have to agree or I won't be a part of any of it." She looked over at Ryan and put her hand on his arm. "I don't understand, Rye. What's changed? I feel like you are hiding something."

He turned his head and closed his eyes. "It's nothing." It looked like he was fighting with himself. When he finally faced her again he said, "Just been difficult at work. I've been under a lot of pressure and I needed the closeness with you." She squeezed his hand in understanding.

"Ryan, do you need me to leave?" Dan asked point-blank. Jenny's jaw dropped at the suggestion. She couldn't bear the thought of losing him.

Rye was silent for several minutes. "No. It's good that Jenny isn't alone when I work late. I'll cut back on my hours once this project is over." He looked at Dan and sighed heavily. "I shouldn't have broken our agreement."

"I accept your apology, but I think I should get a session alone with Jenny. It's only fair."

Ryan frowned. He jumped out of his chair and walked over to the couch, turning on the news. Jenny looked over at Dan, surprised that he was insisting on it. Was it the whole dominant male thing playing out between the two? She could see how letting this slide would only lead to further transgressions, so she kept silent.

After Jenny cleaned the dishes, she joined the guys on the couch. No one spoke as they watched several lame reruns. Finally, Ryan turned off the set and broke the silence. "Okay, you can have one session with Jenny alone, but that's it. Do it tomorrow before I come home. I don't want to dwell on it more than I have to. Keep in mind, I didn't take that long."

"That was your choice, wasn't it?" Dan answered with a raised brow.

Ryan scowled, but said nothing. She knew he was struggling with the consequences of his rash action and her heart went out to him. She suggested that they go to bed early. Jenny felt certain something deeper was going on and she hoped to drag it out of him.

Jenny gave Dan a quick kiss on the cheek and wished him sweet dreams. He grasped the back of her neck and whispered in her ear. "Tomorrow you are all mine." Her insides trembled at the thought. It would be their first time making love alone without any restrictions.

Ryan remained silent as they lay on the bed together. Instead of pressing him further, she laid her head on his chest. "I love you, Rye."

The seconds dragged by before he answered raggedly, "I love you too, Boo."

Time Alone

J enny rushed home a little early the next day. She wanted to be completely clean and ready for Dan. She was shocked to see he'd beaten her there. She laughed aloud when she saw Dan come out of the shower.

"What are you doing home early?"

"I could ask the same of you," he replied, tightening the white towel around his waist.

"I just wanted to freshen up."

"Please do and then join me on the couch." He walked over to her and brushed his lips against hers. He smelled of soap and manly arousal. "Don't take long, I want as much time with you as I can get."

Jenny was a bundle of nerves as she took a quick shower and blow-dried her hair. Even though they'd had sex in every way imaginable, he'd never taken her vaginally alone. Instead, they'd shared that moment with Ryan. Now she was going to experience it as a couple and it made her weak inside.

She put on a virginal-looking white panty and bra set. Jenny turned around in the mirror and giggled in anticipation. She marveled that Dan could make her feel so giddy.

Jenny entered the living room and smiled timidly when she saw him lying on the couch completely naked. He let out a long whistle and beckoned her to him. She was unaware of her feet touching the floor as she made her way to his open arms.

His cock was already fully erect. Obviously, he was as excited about this encounter as she was. "Lie down beside me, like you did the first time."

She settled beside him, her heart beating rapidly. "Do you want me to play with myself?" she asked.

"Of course."

She smiled at him. Unlike the first time, she had no qualms about touching herself while he watched. She slid her fingers under her panties and started rubbing her clit. His fingers joined her under the lace and started playing with her wet outer lips. "Already wet for me?" he growled.

"Always."

His fingers slipped into her opening and stroked her inside as she increased the tempo on her clit. She arched into him and started moaning when his finger found her G-spot. "Oh, Dan…"

"You look so beautiful when you play with yourself," he murmured. It didn't take long before she was writhing and panting. "No need to hold back, baby. Let yourself go."

Jenny turned her head towards him hungrily.

They kissed as her body tensed and then exploded with a sweet orgasm. A gush of liquid escaped when he pulled his fingers away. He licked them and smiled at her. "I love the taste of your come."

She shivered in delight. Dan accepted and loved everything about her. It was an intoxicating feeling.

Her hand snuck over to his crotch and she started stroking his thick member. "Oh no," he said, moving her hand away. "I need to feel myself deep in your wet pussy." He moved off the couch and pointed to the floor. "Will you join me?"

Jenny nodded, peeling off her panties and bra. She lay down on the soft carpet, looking up at Dan. His blond bangs covered his eyes. It was adorable. "Put your arms above your head and spread your legs for me." She did as he asked and he grunted in satisfaction. "You look so damn sexy I could come just looking at you."

No one made her feel as beautiful as Dan did.

He got down in his knees and moved between her legs. She felt his hard cock press against her as he gazed deep into her eyes. She did not break the eye contact as he slowly pushed into her, savoring the feel of his entrance. "You feel so good," she moaned.

Dan braced himself as he started thrusting with more intensity. His shaft caressed her, moving slowly and deliberately. He focused all his attention on her. "Jenny, there's no better place than being deep inside you."

She arched her back and cried out in ecstasy

when the head of his shaft repeatedly caressed her sweet spot. "Will you come with me?" she breathed.

His eyes glowed in lustful agreement. "Kiss me first."

She lifted her head and he pressed his lips against hers as his thrusts changed in tempo. He stroked her at the exact angle to bring her to orgasm. She felt his cock spasm in release, which instantly triggered her own climax. They strained against each other as they succumbed to their mutual fulfillment.

Then she melted onto the carpet and smiled up at him. "You are an amazing lover."

"You inspire me, woman," he growled into her neck. She felt his warm breath on her skin before he began sucking. She moaned as he brought the blood to the surface with his intense suction, knowing he was leaving a mark to answer Ryan's. She wasn't opposed to it. Being marked by her men was sexy, as long as it didn't become an ongoing habit.

He kissed the mark when he was done and then kissed her on the lips. He lifted himself off and picked her up, carrying her to the kitchen table and laying her down on it. "Have you ever had fun with the refrigerator?"

"What do you mean?" She grinned.

"Oh, you're in for a good time, little kumquat." Dan started rifling through the fridge. He brought a chilled bottle of Riesling, a carrot, cucumber, raspberry jam, and a stick of butter. He added a banana from the fruit bowl to his pile. "Just lay there and look beautiful while I get a couple of necessary items."

She looked over at his pile of edible things and shook her head. Leave it to Dan to use food for sexual fun.

He came back with a pack of condoms, lubricant and a naughty glint in his eyes. "Are you ready for a little food play?"

Jenny sat up and sighed nervously. "Dan... if I didn't trust you so much I would say no."

He winked at her. "You know everything I do is for our mutual pleasure. If you don't like anything, just say the word."

She lay back on the table feeling a tad more relaxed. "Have your way with my body then."

The first thing he picked up was the wine. "This will be a little chilly, but we both know you like it cold." He popped off the cork and proceeded to pour a small amount of liquid on her nipple. Jenny jumped when the cold alcohol caressed her skin. Dan's warm lips instantly made contact and he started sucking on her hardened nipple.

"That's nice," she stated. "Almost reminds me of snow."

"Good," he murmured. He poured wine on the opposite breast and let it run down her ribs onto the table. He sucked her nipple and then licked the trail of sweet liquid. He moved further down and gave her a mischievous grin as he poured it on her swollen pussy. She squealed in delight. He lapped up her salty juices along with the sweet wine. "Nice combo," he complimented. Dan picked up the banana and tossed it to her. "Why don't you eat that all sexy-like for me while I go down on you?"

She playfully unpeeled the banana and wrapped her lips around it, slowly inserting it deep into her mouth and then pulling back, she swirled her tongue several times before taking a tiny bite off the tip.

"Oh yeah, baby. That's sexy," he commented and then he went back to sucking on her responsive clit while he watched her. She had fun teasing him, nibbling up the side of it and then peeling back more and taking all of it in her mouth before pulling it back out. He grunted and starting sucking harder in response. She squirmed on the table, having difficulty concentrating on the fruit with his tongue causing pulsing electricity between her legs.

He continued to pour small amounts of cold liquid on her hot sex as he devoured her. It was driving her absolutely crazy. When she finished consuming the banana, she begged him to let her suck his cock.

Dan smiled from between her legs and asked, "Ever lick on a living lollipop?"

She shook her head and giggled as she watched him get a spoonful of raspberry jam. He took it with his fingers and lathered the head of his cock, grunting, "Shit, that's cold." After he cleaned his hands, he joined her on the table, straddling her face in a classic sixty-nine position so that he could resume his attention on her pussy. She took his sticky shaft in her hand and directed it to her mouth. She licked it just like a lollipop. "Yum," she purred. "I love raspberry cock." She kept licking, enjoying the way his manhood warmed the jam and made it all nice and gooey.

She opened her lips and took his full shaft into her mouth, making him groan. He momentarily stopped eating her while he enjoyed her oral attention. She lifted her head up and down, sucking his cock with enthusiasm. She found he tasted extra yummy with the tang of the jam.

After she licked him clean, she began stroking his shaft while she teased the head of his cock with her tongue. She cooed when his precome appeared on the tip, adoring his obvious excitement.

"Okay, enough of that," he growled hoarsely. He crawled off the table and grabbed the stick of butter. She watched him unwrap one end, wondering what on earth he was going to do with it.

"I have never forgotten the feel of your breasts caressing my cock. Would you mind if I indulged a little?"

"My body is all yours," she answered. He rubbed the soft stick of butter liberally over her chest. She looked up at him and giggled. "Do you think this is how they did it in the old days? Grabbed a stick of butter and said, 'Hey, honey, let's have some fun!'"

He kissed her on the lips. "I have no doubt that's how older generations enjoyed themselves." Jenny suddenly had an image of her grandparents playing with a stick of butter and it made her laugh.

Dan positioned himself on her stomach, supporting himself with his legs so he didn't crush her. His cock rested in the valley between her breasts. "Do you remember what to do?"

She nodded as she pressed her breasts around his thick shaft. She had to press hard to completely cover it with her mounds of sexy flesh. He put his hands over hers and started thrusting slowly, watching the action with lustful fascination. "Damn, Jenny. You have the sexiest breasts known to man."

She watched the buttery head of his cock disappear in and out of her cleavage. It turned her on. "Faster, Dan. Fuck my boobs like you mean it."

He groaned and increased the pace of his strokes, but he didn't last long. "Nope. I'm not coming yet, baby. I've got something else in mind." He got off the table and got a towel. With loving tenderness, he cleaned her chest thoroughly. "You don't mind me playing with you like this, do you?"

"No, I love it."

"Okay, I am giving you a choice for this next one." He held up a large straight carrot and the cucumber with a bit of curve to it. "Which one?"

"What are you planning to do with it?"

He just glanced at her pussy and raised an eyebrow.

Her eyes opened wide. "You're going to use a veggie as a dildo?"

"Naturally."

She trembled at the thought and then blushed when she answered, "Cucumber."

"Excellent, I was hoping you would say that."
He surprised her by grabbing a second cucumber
and cutting it into thin slices. He placed a slice in
her mouth. "So you can taste what is making love to
your gorgeous pussy." She loved the flavor of
cucumbers, so fresh and light. He grabbed a con-
dom and rolled it over the large vegetable. Then he
covered it in lubricant. "Spread your legs, baby."

She giggled nervously but did as he asked. Jenny
bit her lip and stared up at the ceiling. He rubbed it
between her swollen lips, letting her feel the width
of it. It was similar in size to his cock and she
wondered if he had picked it out especially for her.

"Arch your back, Jenny." He teased her opening
with the end of it. Unlike his cock, the cucumber
did not give. It was very hard and thick. She moaned
when he started pushing it inside. "That's it. Relax
and let me love you in a new way."

She closed her eyes and felt her body stretch as
the large vegetable slid inside her. Dan guided it in
and out sensually, letting it slowly penetrate her
deeper and deeper. She started rocking her hips to
help with the progress, wondering if she could take
the entire thing. The hard vegetable stretched her
vaginal walls and made her feel delightfully full. She
looked between her legs and watched Dan thrust it
into her. He watched her too, determining which
angle brought her maximum stimulation.

She panted when he found a rhythm and angle
that drove her wild. "Who knew vegetables could be
sexy?" she gasped.

"Anything connected to you is sexy, Jenny." He leaned over and kissed her on the lips with his hand still working the green pseudo-cock. His mouth moved down to her clit and he licked it. "Now I want you to come for me, baby."

She moaned and gave into the unusual experience he was weaving for her. "Yes, Dan. Just like that but faster."

He increased the speed of his tongue and his thrusts. She started to whimper and then a cry escaped her lips as her body creamed the hard vegetable inside her. He groaned as her clit pulsated on his lips and he started stroking his cock. She reached down to help him.

Dan instantly released his suction on her clit and looked up at her. "Don't touch me or I'll explode."

She smiled. "Then explode already."

"Oh no, I want to make love to you again."

Love Deepens

"**C**ome to the office with me." He held out his hand and helped her off the table.

She followed him to the office they had converted into a "bedroom" for Dan. It had a twin bed shoved in the corner. She felt guilty as she looked around and noted that their computer desk pretty much hogged the rest of the tiny room.

He winked at her. "It may not be as big as your bed but trust me, it'll do the job just fine."

"Why don't you lay on that bed and prove it, handsome."

He gave her a sideways grin and settled himself down on the small bed. His cock stood straight and tall, begging to be loved by her. She lay on top of him and pressed her moist outer lips on his rigid member. "Don't move, Dan."

He growled into her ear as she slid her pussy against his cock, not letting him enter her. She covered him thoroughly with her juices. "Feel how wet you make me." She wanted to drag it out, to make him as crazy as he made her. She tilted her hips so that the head of his cock just barely breached her opening. She let it rest there, then she pulled back and let him fall out. "Too soon," she teased.

He groaned in frustration and threw his head back on the pillow. Jenny kissed the center of his chest and sensually glided her lips to his left nipple. She licked and teased it with her teeth and tongue while she adjusted her hips again and let him slip in just a fraction further. She stopped and moved her attention to his right nipple.

He grabbed her waist, ready to thrust himself in deeper, but she commanded, "No, Dan. Put those hands on the bed and take it like a good boy." She pulled away again and his cock slipped out of her moist entrance. "It's my rules."

"You're being so cruel, baby," he complained.

"Sometimes you have to be cruel to be kind." She playfully nipped his chest and then kissed him fully on the lips. He grasped her face and darted his tongue in and the fireworks went off in her head. His kisses had that kind of power over her.

She pushed against him so that the head of his cock penetrated her. Again, she stopped the progress, savoring the feel of just the tip of his shaft inside her fiery walls.

"Woman…" he grumbled through their kiss.

"Be good, handsome. Don't you dare move." She squeezed down on her vaginal muscles, giving him a little massage. He groaned in pleasure and frustration, but stayed still.

Jenny kissed him deeply and then inched his cock in a little further. He stiffened, obviously hoping she would keep going, but she was feeling wicked so she let him slip all the way out and slid her wet pussy over the length of his cock again.

"Baby, please…"

"You are being such a good boy, maybe I *should* reward you," she purred. Jenny wanted him deep inside her, probably more than he did. She shifted her hips and his shaft slid into her seamlessly and they both groaned.

She looked down at him, attempting to keep a serious expression. "Now I want you to just lay there. Let me take that big cock of yours at my own pace." He nodded his head, looking down at his cock slowly disappearing into her moist heaven.

Jenny placed her hands on his chest and rocked back on his cock ever so slightly. She was making exquisite torture for them both. With patience she hadn't known she possessed, she pushed his manhood in slowly, loving how his shaft became a part of her.

Once he was buried deep inside, she looked down at Dan and smiled. "Now you can move."

His eyes flashed with excitement as he grabbed onto her hips. But instead of thrusting hard and fast like she expected, he pushed into her with tenderness, moving her up and down slowly on his cock. He looked into her eyes and whispered, "I love everything about you."

Her heart threatened to burst. She leaned down and kissed him again. "I love you too, Dan. So much it almost hurts."

He pressed her against his chest as they moved in unison together, expressing their emotions through their lovemaking. The buildup was slow and intense. She concentrated on the feel of him, the way his shaft adored her on the inside as his hands expressed his love over her skin.

"Don't ever stop loving me," she whispered.

"I won't," he assured her, brushing back her hair to look into her eyes. "I will always love you."

She cried when she came. Jenny laid her head back on his chest, the feeling of love overwhelming. She held her breath when his seed released inside her. Somehow, it made her complete.

"Oh baby, baby..." he murmured, hugging her closer to him.

They lay there intertwined for a long time. It was a beautiful feeling she never wanted to end. But soon, she heard the front door and knew Ryan was home earlier than usual.

There was no hiding what they had done with her underwear strewn in the living room, foods items used and abused in the kitchen, and the two of them coming out of the office completely naked.

"You're home early," Dan said in a deadpan voice, trying to keep things light.

Ryan looked at them both and Jenny couldn't miss the slight wince. She hated him to feel left out.

"I'm glad you're home!" she said, throwing her arms around his middle and pressing her naked body against him.

He tried to push her away. "I'm not looking for a pity fuck."

Jenny looked up at him and shook her head. "I would never! No, when I fuck you it's all about love." She started unzipping his pants and knelt down between his legs. When he didn't stop her, she released his shaft from the confines of his briefs and started sucking. Ryan ran his hands through her hair, but remained silent.

She heard Dan in the kitchen, probably cleaning up the evidence of their fun. He came back with a glass of warm Riesling for each of them. "You can keep doing what you're doing, I just hate to see a good wine go to waste."

"Thanks," Ryan said, sounding far more relaxed. He took a drink and then looked down at her. "Why don't we move this to the couch?" He helped her up and they clinked glasses together.

"Here's to you *coming* home, Rye." Jenny said light-heartedly.

Ryan winked at her and settled down on the couch. She put her glass down and disappeared between his legs again, reveling in his manliness. His shaft grew hard and long in her mouth as she lavished her love on him. Then she took his balls in her mouth one at a time, sucking lightly.

"Damn it, Boo. I could come in that lovely mouth of yours."

"Feel free," she said, looking up at him lustfully. Jenny took his cock back into her mouth, hoping he would let her taste his essence for the first time. It looked like he was contemplating it, but then he changed his mind.

"No. How can I when your pussy calls to me? I want to take you doggy style."

Ryan got off the couch and Dan took his place. She was disappointed Rye had chickened out, but happily took Dan in her mouth as she spread her legs and arched her back.

Rye moved behind and eased his dick into her. She moaned on Dan's cock as Ryan pushed in deep. He held onto her waist and began stroking long and hard. "God, I love the feel of your hot pussy."

She had trouble sucking Dan properly with the hard pounding Ryan was giving her, so she switched to stroking his cock and licking the head of his shaft randomly. Dan didn't seem to mind as he played with her bouncing tits.

Ryan slowed down his strokes and caressed her buttocks. "You have the sexiest butt, Jen." He grabbed a round cheek in each hand and squeezed. "I think it's why I love this position so much. I can't get enough of this ass jiggling when you take my pounding." He growled deeply and resumed his hard thrusts.

Jenny purred. The angle was particularly delicious. She stroked Dan's cock harder in response to her own pleasure. In turn, Dan ran his hands over her back and shoulders appreciatively. Then he winked and said in a low, barely audible voice, "Go ahead, concentrate on Ryan. I'll just sit here and watch." She kissed the head of his cock before putting her hands on the couch to brace herself better.

She started pushing against Ryan's thrusts to drive him in deeper. He grunted loudly, "Oh fuck…"

Jenny moaned as she met each of his strokes, but she wanted more. "Give it to me, Rye. Don't hold back."

He surprised her by fingering her asshole. "I could come just touching you like this," he growled between his teeth. Having Ryan play with her that way while pounding her was an exciting variation he'd never tried before.

He put more muscle behind his pelvic thrusts as his thumb slowly circled her rim and then pushed into her tight hole. She cried out, "Ooohhh, that feels good…"

"Damn it, Jen. You're making me come." He stiffened inside her and pushed deep as he climaxed. She purred in delight, loving the ability to make him lose control like that. He complained good-naturedly as he pulled out, "Shame on you, that was too fast. I think you should be punished." He looked over at Dan. "Let's take her to the bed and tease her until she comes."

Dan grinned. "Sounds like a plan." He walked with her to the bedroom while Ryan went to wash his hands. The two settled on either side of Jenny with Ryan concentrating on her breasts. Dan focused on teasing her humming pussy.

Rye pinched and rolled her nipple with his fingers as he suckled her breasts with relish. She looked at his crotch and was surprised to see that his cock was already hardening so soon after coming. It amazed her that her breasts had that kind of effect on him.

Dan's fingers played with her moist inner folds. He didn't concentrate on her clit, instead he tortured it, playing around the area but never touching it—making her poor body wild for more. She started squirming in frustration.

Dan told Ryan, "I think we need to hold her down."

Both men grabbed a wrist and continued their sexual torture. Jenny cried out in protest, which only spurred them to be crueler. They ramped up the stimulation, Ryan sucking harder and Dan continually caressing her clit with a light frustrating touch. She wiggled her hips in desperation. "Please…" she whimpered.

"She's begging for it. Should we take pity on her?" Ryan asked.

"Why not?" Dan answered with a smirk.

"I want to be the one to bring her to orgasm," Ryan insisted.

"Fine, then I'll kiss her as she comes." Dan looked at her with luminous eyes. "I love kissing your lips as your inner lips contract in pleasure."

Jenny moaned softly as Ryan inserted two fingers inside her and began stroking her G-spot. She pushed her head back on the pillow and closed her eyes. Her heart rate doubled as her body responded to his practiced touch. Ryan now knew exactly how to play her body to a satisfying climax.

Dan's lips landed on hers. He kissed her deeply as her mound bucked against Ryan's hand. She groaned into his mouth when the orgasm threatened to crash over her.

"That's it, Jen. Feel my love for you," Ryan whispered as he slowly fingered her G-spot. "Let it transform into pleasure."

She stopped fighting the huge wave and allowed it to consume her. Her whole body tensed just before the explosion. She had to break her kiss with Dan because it was so intense. Jenny gasped as her body pumped Ryan's fingers.

"Damn, you're beautiful to watch," Dan said, nibbling on her ear.

"Nothing beats actually feeling her pussy's climax," Ryan answered, as he pulled his fingers out and lovingly caressed her still-pulsing clit.

Dan smiled. "I'll take either, or both. I'm not picky."

Jenny noticed that both men had raging hard-ons. "Can I tell you what I want?"

"Naturally," Ryan answered, his hand slowly moving from her mound up to her nipples, covering them in her own juices.

Dan bent over and kissed her nipple and then sucked on it. It was so erotic that she shivered and lost her train of thought for a second. "I want to suck both your cocks."

Dan's eyes lit up, but Ryan looked at her cautiously. Jenny understood his reservation and tried to assure him, "Rye, I want to taste your come, please."

She got off the bed and kneeled on the floor, both men standing on either side of her. She took Ryan's long thin cock and Dan's stout thick one and started stroking their rock-hard members at the same time. Then she leaned over to lick and nibble on one before turning her attention on the other. It was exciting having control of two cocks at the same time, making her men wait for their turn with her mouth.

Dan and Ryan both watched her intently, hunger radiating from their eyes. She glanced up at them, slowly taking Ryan's cock in her mouth while she stroked Dan's with vigor. Rye played with her midnight hair, groaning under his breath. She popped him out of her mouth and started on Dan, caressing Ryan's shaft in a rolling motion. Both men cried out, causing Jenny to suck and stroke with more enthusiasm.

"This won't take long," Dan groaned.

"Tell me when you're ready and I'll stick my tongue out so you both can bathe it," she said, her voice ripe with anticipation.

She directed her attention back on Ryan, determined to get him to orgasm at the same time as Dan. She sucked hard and moaned on his shaft. He grabbed her head and pushed her further on his dick and then announced, "Oh yeah, I'm coming."

She pulled away and opened her mouth wide, sticking out her tongue to catch his seed. Dan moved beside her and put his hand over hers so that together they stroked his shaft. Both men's cocks erupted with white gold. She moaned in pleasure as they covered her tongue with their essence. She swallowed several times, not wanting to miss a drop, but there was too much and some dripped from her chin onto her chest.

Ryan bent down and pressed his forehead against hers. "Thank you…"

She purred, "No, thank you. I've wanted to do that forever."

"I guess I'm an idiot for waiting so long."

Jenny smiled up at Ryan lovingly. "Well, you're an idiot no longer."

Kelly's Revenge

Despite his promise, Ryan's hours did not decrease after the project ended. He stayed late into the night as the weeks progressed, coming home exhausted and drained. "Rye, you have to stop killing yourself. You can't keep this up forever," Jenny told him, concerned for his mental and physical health.

"I'm so close to making junior partner I can taste it, Jen! I don't care what it takes. Soon you'll be looking at the next junior partner."

"But you know I don't care about that. I just want my Rye back."

Ryan glared at her. "What do you mean you don't care? You know this is important to me. To *us*."

She wrapped her arms around him. "I never cared about you becoming junior partner. You're the only one who cares about that stuff. All I want is to spend quality time with you."

He shook himself from her embrace angrily. "I'm doing this for us and you act like it's nothing. Like it doesn't even matter."

She rolled her eyes playfully, ignoring his outburst. "You know what they say, all work and no play…"

"I expect your support, Jenny. I don't appreciate you undermining me like this." He stalked off to the bedroom and slammed the door behind him.

Jenny looked over at Dan with tears in her eyes. "I'm losing him. He's going back to the old Ryan."

"He's under a lot of pressure right now."

"Of his own making!" she snapped. "He doesn't have to work such awful hours."

Dan said calmly, "He's doing it for you."

"No, he says he is doing it for me, but I would rather have Rye here and he knows it." Jenny was so frustrated that she grabbed her purse and headed out of the apartment. She ended up at a playground nearby, sitting on a swing with a single streetlight shining down on her. She appreciated the calming effect swinging had on her. It helped her to think more clearly.

A part of her resented that Ryan didn't care how his long hours affected her. In a way, Dan was a crutch for him. Ryan could work as late as he wanted without feeling guilty about it. What he didn't take into account was that the intimate times she craved with him were becoming few and far between. The current situation wasn't working for her. Once he became junior partner she was certain it would only get worse.

When she returned home, she'd hoped to talk to Ryan but found him asleep in bed. She undressed and joined him. She was shocked how lonely she felt lying beside Rye. She snuggled up and tried to regain their connection. Her heart froze when he heard him whisper in his sleep, "Kelly…"

Jenny distanced herself from him. Why would he say *her* name? She spent the night staring at the ceiling telling herself repeatedly that it was nothing.

She didn't speak to him about it the next morning, but insisted on having lunch together. Ryan complained that he didn't have the time, but she would not take no for an answer.

They met at a restaurant close to his office. It meant an extra twenty minutes of travel time for her, but she was willing to make the sacrifice. Even so, Ryan was ten minutes late. She squelched her anger when he finally showed up and sat down across from her.

"Well, you got me here. What do you want?" he said unenthusiastically, looking at his watch.

She chose not to beat around the bush. "You said Kelly's name in your sleep last night." He rubbed his chin, but offered no reply. She wasn't going to let his lack of response deter her. "I've felt for quite some time that you were hiding something from me."

"It's nothing."

Her lip trembled. "Don't lie to me, Ryan. Why would you say her name?"

He sighed and opened up the menu to avoid looking at her. "Kelly has called me on several occasions, but it's not important."

She slammed the menu down. "Not important! This is the same woman who hit me with her car."

"Kelly was desperate to apologize about that, so she called me. It turns out it was just an accident. When she hit you, she immediately pulled away. That's probably why the cop didn't see her."

"And you buy that story?" Jenny felt a churning in her stomach. "Rye, I don't believe her, not for a second. And I don't understand why you are talking to her."

"Look, she's the one calling me."

"Yes, but you don't have to answer the calls."

He gave her a look she couldn't read and then he said in a low whisper, "I don't think you realize how much your actions devastated her. She is not as strong as I am. You and Dan really hurt her, Jen."

Jenny cringed, knowing it was true. "I never meant to…"

"Regardless, she needed someone to talk to who understands. No one can relate unless they've been through it," he replied with an undertone of resentment. "I've been trying to help her cope."

It pissed Jenny off that Kelly was talking to Ryan. Couldn't he see she was only trying to cause trouble between them? "When was the last time she called you?" Jenny demanded.

"Yesterday. It's probably why I said her name last night." He could obviously see her distrust because he added, "Jen, there is nothing going on. You don't need to worry."

Her eyes narrowed in suspicion and resentment. "If that's true, why would you keep it a secret from me?"

Ryan patted her hand as if she were a child. "I didn't see any point in upsetting you over nothing."

She grasped his hands in both of hers and held them tightly. "But we promised not to keep anything from each other."

He stared at their hands intertwined together and looked as if he was contemplating saying more. Instead, he gazed into her eyes. She swore his jade eyes held a secret she wasn't privy to.

"Talk to me, Rye."

He closed his eyes and turned away. "You know what? I don't have time for this. You can order anything you like, but I really need to get back to the office."

Ryan didn't even wait for her to reply. He got up and spoke to the waitress, leaving Jenny alone at the table. The tears fell onto her empty plate. The waitress came up and explained that Ryan had taken care of the bill. When Jenny didn't reply, the kind-hearted women refilled her glass of water and told her to take as much time as she needed.

She didn't stay. Jenny gathered her things and ran out of the restaurant. She thought she saw Kelly disappear around the corner as she made her way out. *Is that bitch stalking us?*

Jenny returned to work a jumble of nerves. She

couldn't concentrate and asked to leave early. She was shocked to find Ryan waiting at home when she got there.

"Hey, Jen. Sorry about lunch. I've been thinking about what you said last night." He wrapped his arms around her waist. "I've not been here for you." He lifted her chin. "And I miss playing with you, too."

She relaxed in his arms. "It feels like it's been ages." He kissed her just as Dan entered the apartment.

"I take it you guys have kissed and made up?"

Ryan answered huskily, "More than that. I've come home early for a little ménage."

Dan grinned. "Excellent! Let me go clean up and I will join you guys in a few. Feel free to warm up without me."

Ryan took her face in his hands. "My little Cherokee hottie." He pulled her towards the bedroom and sat on the bed, drawing her closer. "Let me undress you." He lifted off her blouse and removed her bra to lick her already hard nipples. He looked at her seductively and asked, "Can I tell you what I've been dreaming about for ages?"

"What, Rye?"

"My long dick sliding down your throat." She felt a tingling in her loins at the suggestion. She hadn't done it in such a long time, but the fact Ryan desired it turned her on. He muttered as he went back to tease her nipple, "I was jealous of Dan when I saw you take him that way."

His last statement concerned her, but she hoped tonight would ease any feelings of jealousy. "I want to make that dream come true…"

"Good," he groaned, taking her nipple back into his mouth and sucking hard. His fingers made their way under the waistband of her damp panties. "You're wet for me, aren't you?"

"Yes," she whispered. She played with his mop of brown curls while he lavished his attention on her breasts.

Dan joined them in the bedroom and Jenny explained what was about to happen. Ryan continued to suck on her breasts as Dan pulled at her remaining clothes. She felt his warm tongue lick the length of her slit while his hands caressed her buttocks. He didn't have free access to her, so he suggested she lie on the bed.

She put her head on the edge of the bed and spread her legs open for Dan, wanting him to continue licking her pussy while she readied herself to deepthroat Ryan.

Dan instructed him, "Let her suck on your shaft until she's ready. She'll need to build up plenty of saliva, it's normal and necessary."

Ryan surprised Jenny when he barked, "I know, Dan. I saw her do it with you."

"Hey, just trying to help." Dan disappeared between her legs and began sucking on her clit, creating the slow burn Jenny enjoyed.

She took Ryan's long shaft and started playing with the head first, teasing and nibbling it. He groaned in appreciation. "Oh yeah, that's hot." He started thrusting his shaft deeper, but she stopped him with her hand.

"No, Rye. I decide how deep."

"Yeah," he agreed huskily.

She continued her teasing, slowly taking his long member deeper. She wondered how Ryan's long shaft would feel compared to Dan's thicker one. When the head of his cock brushed against the back of her throat, she took a break. She focused instead on Dan's talented tongue *and* his magic fingers that had her pussy aching for more.

Jenny reminded herself that she needed to swallow. She'd forgotten to do that the first time she tried to deepthroat Dan and it caused a lot of gagging. She looked up at Ryan seductively. "Are you ready for me to love you with my throat?"

He grunted in answer and moved his cock back into her wide-open lips. She took him in slowly and swallowed hard when he reached the back. She felt his shaft start traveling down her throat. Thinner proved much easier to take and she moaned in satisfaction.

Ryan cried out lustfully, making her loins gush. It thrilled her to be giving this part of herself to him. His cock was much longer and she got to a point where she needed to push him back out. She put her hands on his hips and tried to disengage, but he was lost in the feeling. Instead of pulling out, he pushed himself in deeper with a thrusting motion. Her throat constricted around his cock as she struggled to breathe. Jenny panicked and started pushing hard against him.

Dan shouted and suddenly Ryan was out. She rolled into a ball and started coughing and gasping for air, tears running down her face.

"I'm sorry, Jen," Ryan exclaimed.

Dan was beside her, rubbing her back soothingly as he yelled at Ryan. "What the hell were you thinking? You don't force yourself! You *never* force yourself."

"Shut the fuck up, Dan! I am so tired of you telling me what to do." Ryan tried to touch her, but Jenny instinctually moved away from him. He raged at Dan, "This is your fault!"

"My fault? I'm not the idiot who hurt Jenny!"

"It was a fucking accident."

"Oh yeah, grabbing her head and thrusting is an *accident.*"

"That's it!" Ryan seized Dan's arm and pushed him out of their bedroom. The shouting match continued in the living room.

Jenny was powerless to stop it. She lay there in a shaking heap, slowly regaining her breath. Her throat hurt and the panic she felt still haunted her. She heard the door slam and eventually Ryan returned to the bedroom.

"I never meant to hurt you, Jen. I wish I could take it back." He sat on the edge of the bed and did not make a move towards her.

"It really hurt."

He hung his head. "I don't know what to say

other than I'm sorry."

Dark silence shrouded the room. She remained in a fetal position, hugging herself. "Where's Dan?" she finally asked.

"I told him to pack his bags."

She lifted her head up. "What! Why?"

"This wouldn't have happened if he hadn't been here."

She sat up in the bed and wrapped herself in the sheet. "This isn't his fault!" she protested.

"I never would have tried to deepthroat you if it wasn't for Dan."

"You're the one who wanted to try it. I don't understand how you can blame him for this."

"Don't you see? Kelly is right, Dan is tearing us apart. He is trying to ruin what you and I have."

"What are you talking about? He is the best thing to happen to us. You've become a better lover because of him."

Ryan's face turned a deep shade of red and he snarled, "What? I wasn't good enough for you before?"

She stared him down without saying anything.

"Damn it, Jen! If you hadn't played into his hands and let him have his way with you, we wouldn't be here right now. This is his fault plain and simple. *He* is the wedge between us."

"Ryan, things can never go back to the way they were. I love Dan. You know that!"

"And what about me?"

She hesitated before she answered. "I love

you..."

"But what?" he demanded.

"Ryan..." She looked down, unable to look him in the eye. "I don't really trust you right now."

"Because of what happened tonight? Come on, Jen. It was a mistake. It'll never happen again."

"It's not just that. You never told me about Kelly. You were hiding it from me...from *us*."

"I don't owe Dan anything. The only one I care about is you." He became visibly agitated. "Don't you see? Dan's the problem here. Kelly told me she is willing to forgive you if you end it with Dan."

"The fact you are speaking to her at all feels like a betrayal." Jenny got up and dressed, grabbing an overnight bag. She stuffed it haphazardly, unable to focus. "I need time alone."

"Wait. Where are you going?"

"I don't know, but I need to get out of here." She collected a few things from the bathroom and headed towards the door.

"Jen, don't go!" She heard the desperation in his voice, but the anger she felt towards him closed up her already sore throat. She grabbed her car keys and ran out the door without looking back.

The Cabin

Jenny started driving, not having a clue where she was headed. She couldn't understand how the night had gone from a playful interlude to this. She cranked up her tunes and let the tears fall. She couldn't wrap her mind around the fact that Ryan had hurt her on top of lying about Kelly.

After driving for an hour, she realized she was in the foothills headed towards Dan's family cabin. She hoped they wouldn't mind if she spent the night there.

The cabin was dark when she pulled up. She remembered fondly how it looked buried in snow with the trail of smoke flowing from the chimney. She hefted her bag on her shoulder and located the key under the porch. When she opened the door, she was assaulted with the smell of stale smoke. She figured no one had aired the place out after the two of them were snowed in together.

Luckily, the electricity was back. She flicked on

the lights and looked around, noticing that the place was exactly the same as they left it all those months ago. There was even a can of Vienna sausages still on the counter. She went over and popped it open, suddenly aware that she was hungry.

The pile of firewood still lined one side of the cabin wall. She picked up a couple of logs and started a fire. The warm glow set her mind at ease. She grabbed a blanket off one of the beds and brought it to the couch. She lay down and wrapped herself in the fuzzy cover, staring at the flames. It calmed her. Being here brought a sense of home. She sighed and snuggled deeper into the blanket. On the coffee table sat the deck of cards. She smiled, remembering Dan's game of strip poker.

Ryan was right; she had played into Dan's hands willingly. Maybe not at first, but there was a spark she could not deny. Even though their affair had wreaked havoc on both their lives, she didn't regret it. For a brief period of time, the three of them had been happy—truly happy.

Now it was over, Kelly had seen to that. Just as Jenny had willingly played into Dan's hands, Ryan had done the same with Kelly. Jenny could just imagine Kelly systematically breaking down Ryan's defenses until he started questioning the beautiful relationship the three had created.

Where did that leave her now? A huge yawn escaped her lips. Now was not the time to decide. Tomorrow, after a good night's rest, she would have a better perspective. She let the fire die down and drifted off to sleep.

She awoke to the sound of the cabin door opening and screamed out in fear.

"It's okay, Jenny. It's just me."

Dan turned on the lights. She had to blink several times before she could make out more than his outline. He carried a bag of groceries and his own overnight bag. "I had no idea you would be here until I saw your car parked outside."

"I didn't think your family would mind," she said defensively. "I needed a place to stay for one night."

"It's fine." He put his stuff down on the counter and walked over to her. "What happened with Ryan?"

"I'd rather not talk about it right now."

He headed to the kitchenette. "Okay. We can talk in the morning. Let me get this stuff put away and you can go back to sleep." He threw the groceries in the fridge and started the fire back up. He turned off the lights and joined her on the couch. She made room so that they were lying side-by-side watching the flames lick the pieces of wood.

Despite the emotional day, the hypnotic character of the fire and the warmth of his embrace helped her drift off to sleep. She felt safe with his arms wrapped around her, she always had.

Jenny didn't wake until morning when she felt him shifting. "Go back to sleep," he murmured.

She couldn't, so she lay there and watched him. Dan reignited the fire and started brewing coffee.

While it dripped, he scrambled eggs and browned the bacon. Soon the little cabin was filled with the aromatic smell of strong coffee and smoked bacon. He laid the feast on the table and motioned to her.

"Come join me for some needed sustenance. Something tells me you survived on Vienna sausages last night and that won't do."

She smiled and wrapped the blanket around her as she made her way to the table. She couldn't help thinking of their snowy interlude on that same piece of furniture. She blushed when she sat down. "Thanks, Dan."

They ate in silence. Finally, he asked, "So what happened after I left?"

"Ryan blamed you for everything. Kelly made sure of that."

"So he's been in contact with her?"

"Yes. For a while now, apparently. I just found out yesterday. If you can believe, Ryan has this crazy idea that everything can go back to the way it was without you."

"Kelly is a convincing manipulator. He was a fool to listen to her and a bigger fool to keep it a secret from us."

"I swear I saw her outside the restaurant yesterday after I met with Ryan. I'm afraid she might be stalking him."

"Don't worry about Ryan. He can take care of himself. It's only you I'm worried about."

"But Dan, she's ruined everything! It can never be like it was these past few months."

"No, that part of our lives is over," he said solemnly. He put his fork down and stared at her. "What are you planning to do, Jenny?"

She pushed her plate away and looked at him sadly. "I've finally come to realize something I've been blind to for years." Her lip trembled slightly. "Ryan and I don't want the same thing. He's always been dead set on advancing in his job, but I hate the hours. I didn't realize how much because I'd grown accustomed to being alone most of the time... until you came into my life. I don't want to go back to that lifestyle, spending my life waiting for someone to come home."

"He wants to provide for you," Dan said in his best friend's defense.

"I don't care about the money, I never have."

He got up and collected her plate, taking them both to the sink to rinse. "So are you thinking about leaving him?" he asked as the water trickled slowly out of the faucet.

Jenny's heart rate shot up. It was the million-dollar question. She finally understood that their lives were not compatible, even though she loved Ryan. It was clear to her now. "Ryan needs a woman who can appreciate his drive to succeed in the business world. The fact is I am not that woman."

Dan turned towards her, his hair covering his eyes. He brushed it back all cute-like. "What does that mean for us?"

Jenny stood up and walked over to him. She put

her hands on his chest and gazed into his dark brown eyes. "I love you, Dan. I want to be with you."

He wrapped her in a tight embrace. "God, how I have wanted to hear you say that." His voice was gruff with emotion.

Jenny rested her head against his firm chest and a feeling of peace enveloped her. She had found her home. This time there was no second-guessing her desire. She loved Dan—mind, body and soul.

He pulled away and grabbed her hand, heading towards the door. "Come with me."

"But I don't have shoes on," she complained.

"You won't need them. It's not far." Dan led her outside to the large pine that stood in front of the cabin. She tiptoed her way through the tiny rocks and pine needles, giggling as he smiled down at her. His eyes held a sparkle she only seen once before—the day she had shouted that she loved him in the cabin.

Dan pointed to the large Blue Spruce. "My great-grandparents planted this tree after they built the cabin. It has special significance to me because my dad proposed to my mom under its branches. He even carved their initials in the trunk." Dan lovingly caressed the scars on the bark. She touched the outline of the heart with her finger.

Jenny felt a nervous tingling course through her body when he took her hand. "Jenny, I would like to continue that tradition." She looked into his eyes, suddenly unable to breathe. He gently cupped her cheek. "Will you be my wife?"

Her whole body quivered at his touch. "Dan..."

"I love you, woman. I don't want to share you anymore. I want you all to myself. Forever."

She pressed her hand against his and said with tears in her eyes, "That sounds wonderful."

He took a deep breath and asked, "Is that a yes then?"

She took his hand and kissed it tenderly. "Yes."

Dan picked her up and lifted her high above him, turning in circles. "She said yes!" he shouted, and the mountains echoed back their reply. He brought her back to earth and kissed her fiercely. "*My* woman."

She grabbed his waist, pressing herself against him. "*My* man."

He smiled down at her and then pulled a pocketknife out from his jeans. Dan set to the task of marking the tree with their initials on the other side of the tree trunk. As she watched, she could just imagine one of their children doing the same years from now. It was surreal... and wonderful.

When he was finished, he stood back and asked, "What do you think, Jenny?"

She ran her finger over the fresh cuts. "It's beautiful."

He folded the pocketknife and then picked her up, carrying her back into the cabin. He set her on the couch and sat down beside her. "You realize this officially marks the beginning of our lives together."

She snuggled up closer to him. "Funny that it

took a blizzard to set us on the right path."

He kissed the top of her head. "Nature seems to have a wisdom all her own."

They sat there in pleasant silence. After a while, however, his closeness called to her. He must have felt it too because he leaned over and growled softly in her ear, "So Jenny, have you ever…"

Blissfully Taken

J enny awoke, but kept her eyes closed. His hand was playing with her breast using feather-light caresses. When it started traveling south and tickled her stomach, she giggled and opened her eyes. His dark brown eyes smiled down at her. "Morning, Kumquat."

"Ah... Dan, I like this."

"What?"

"Waking up to your face."

He chuckled. "More than just my face, my love." Dan's fingers moved between her legs and began the light caress of her dark mound. He started off slow, waking her body gently to his lust.

Jenny opened her legs to him and turned her head into his chest, breathing in his masculine scent. What a way to start the morning.

He spread her wetness over her sex so his fingers could slide easily over her clit. She pressed against his hand and moaned softly. The fire was starting deep within. When she tried to reposition to return the favor, he whispered, "Don't move. Just enjoy."

She lay back and let Dan weave his spell of passion. His fingers glided over her folds, flicking her clit, moving to her opening to tease the rim. She shifted as the tension grew; Dan knew her body so well it was uncanny.

He penetrated her with two fingers and began stroking her G-spot. Jenny groaned as her hips naturally tilted in response to the stimulation. His fingers swirled around that sweet spot, taking away any chance of control for her. Her clit started pulsing in pleasure. "Dan," she breathed.

"Yes, Jenny?" he growled into her ear.

"Aaaah—" Her voice cut off as she was overcome by the sweet climax he created. She pressed her lips against his chest as it rolled over her.

"Nothing sexier than watching you come," he said as he pulled his fingers from her and lightly spread the wetness on his fingers over her skin. Dan had a way of making her feel sexy and perfect, as if every part of her was to be treasured.

"I love you." She adored saying those little three words.

He kissed her on her forehead. "I love you too, woman."

Jenny suddenly felt a stab in her heart. She buried her head in the pillow, willing it away—not wanting it to ruin the moment.

There was no hiding it from Dan, he knew her

too well. "Yes. We have to tell Ryan today. He deserves to be told the truth as soon as possible."

"This will crush him," she whimpered into the pillow.

"Ryan has been pulling away for a while now, Jenny. I do not think this will come as a surprise."

"I don't know, Dan…"

"Do you want to tell him together?"

"No, I need to do this alone."

"Well, I will have my cell phone with me. If at any point you want me there, just call."

"It won't be necessary."

"Still, know I won't be far away."

She sighed miserably. A pit in her stomach was growing larger with each passing minute. "I'd better go after breakfast, I guess. The sooner the better."

He brushed back a tendril of her black hair from her cheek. "I agree. It would be better for all of us."

Jenny headed out as soon as breakfast was over. She might as well have skipped the meal since her stomach was tied in knots and she couldn't eat a thing.

"I'm near if you need me," Dan reminded her, before he got into his own car.

Jenny drove back to the city, trembling the entire drive. How would Ryan take the news that she was marrying Dan? That she was ending their relationship of almost four years? She hoped that Dan was right and that Ryan would see this coming. If not, it was going to be a heartbreaking confrontation.

Jenny stood at the door, afraid to announce her arrival. Normally she would just walk in, but now everything had changed. She held her breath as she rang the doorbell and waited. The door swung open as if he was expecting her.

Ryan pulled Jenny into his embrace and groaned, "You came back!"

"Rye…"

He ushered her inside and shut the door. "Sit down. Tell me what you are thinking."

She looked into his jade-colored eyes. She hated that she was about to bring pain to those familiar eyes. "I've been with Dan."

Ryan pushed away from her and sat on the other end of the couch. "Why would you do that?"

"It wasn't planned, we both ended up at the cabin."

Anguish clouded his gaze. "The cabin."

"I came back today to tell you in person—"

He put his hand out to silence her, standing up abruptly. "I don't want to hear it. You need some time to calm down. You aren't thinking clearly right now."

She stood up slowly and walked over to him. "Ryan, Dan and I—"

Ryan yelled at her, "I don't want to hear it! That fucking Dan, as soon as he saw the chance…"

Jenny would not be swayed. "Ryan, we are getting married. Dan proposed yesterday."

"Damn him to hell!" Ryan turned on her. "You take it back. You are not marrying that motherfucker. Do you hear me?"

She stepped away from him. "I'm sorry, Ryan, but—"

"Don't say it. Don't you fucking say that to me! You and Dan, all this time… playing me for a fool. Kelly was right."

Jenny returned the fire. "Don't you understand? Kelly did this! You let Kelly do this to us. It was perfect, the three of us together. But you let her ruin what we had."

Ryan rammed his palm into her chest and pushed her up against the wall. His voice was deadly calm in its hatred. "You are to blame, not Kelly. I will never forgive you for this betrayal."

"My betrayal? You've been siding up with Kelly for God knows how long, and you hurt me two days ago." She added with a snarl, "Just like you are doing now."

He did not loosen his grip, laughing angrily. "Oh, that's it. Blame me. I bet you and Dan talked about me the whole time you were up at the cabin. Putting me down, laughing at my expense."

"It's not like that. It has never been like that. Dan's your best friend."

Ryan pressed harder against her, hissing, "Don't… ever… call him that again."

Jenny struggled to breathe until he finally let go and she gasped for air.

"I hate you, Jenny."

She wanted to protest, to say something to preserve their relationship on some level, but there was nothing that could fix it. Jenny turned away from Ryan and headed towards the door.

"Don't go."

She hesitated when she put her hand on the doorknob.

"Stay, please."

Jenny sighed. "Ryan, it won't change anything."

His voice cracked. "I need you."

Jenny closed her eyes. This was Ryan, the man she had dated since college, the man she had planned to marry once—the man she still cared about. She turned around and sat down when he motioned her to the couch.

"Good," he stated. "We've been here before. You get mixed up when you are around Dan. It takes distance away from him for you to think straight."

She was about to disagree, but he put his finger to her lips. "No, don't say anything. Listen." He put his hand down and continued, "I have loved you longer than Dan. I have loved you through good times and bad. You will never find someone as loyal as I am. I forgave your transgression with Dan. I misspoke out of anger earlier, I *will* forgive you now. However, this has to stop. You are not allowed to see that asshole again. Ever."

She shook her head. "You aren't listening to me. I'm marrying Dan. I already said yes and nothing you say will change that."

Ryan growled under his breath. "You are an idiot. He will leave you high and dry like he left Kelly.

He doesn't love you. He is incapable of love, or friendship for that matter."

"Dan loves me, Ryan, and I love him. I wish it was different. I wish the three of us could have made it work. But you pushed us away."

"I didn't change. You did."

Jenny looked down at her lap and fiddled with the hem of her skirt. "Maybe we both did."

"We'll go back to the way it was. I am willing to start over, just the two of us."

Silence dragged on for an uncomfortably long time before she finally braved an answer. "Well, I'm not."

Ryan shot off the couch. "Damn you to hell, Jenny! I have given you everything. Everything! How can you treat me so callously when all I have ever been is kind? Are you a fucking whore? Is Kelly right about you?"

Jenny narrowed her eyes. "Kelly. It always comes back to Kelly. She is playing you like a puppet and you don't even see it."

"No!" he screamed. "You played me, Dan played me." Ryan paced around the room in a state of rage Jenny had never thought he was capable of. "God, I hate you! But fuck it all…" His face crumpled. "I still love you."

Jenny's heart broke for Ryan. He loved her, he always had. He'd proven it at the cabin when he took her back, then later when he brought Dan into their relationship, but if she had to make a choice it would always be Dan.

"Rye…" She saw the hope rise in his eyes and realized she had to release him now. It would hurt both of them, but it was necessary to move forward. "I care about you. I always will, but I am marrying Dan."

He fell to his knees. It shocked Jenny. She moved to comfort him and had to stop herself.

Ryan looked at her in desperation. "Don't."

Her lips trembled as she turned towards the door. There was nothing more to say. She needed to get out of there.

"Boo."

Jenny looked back at him with tears in her eyes.

He held his hand out to her. "Don't leave me."

She opened the door and rushed out, her heart breaking into a million pieces. She ran to her car and took off, but she pulled over a block away and cried. She howled in pain—hating herself, hating what she had done.

It wasn't until she heard her cell phone that she came back to reality. She sobbed several times before answering Dan's call.

"Jenny, are you all right?"

She could barely gasp out the words. "No, Dan. I am not."

"Did anything happen? Are you hurt?" he asked in concern.

"Yes, something happened. I broke Ryan's heart. He didn't see it coming. I feel awful."

"I'm sorry, Jenny. I'm sorry he took it so hard, but it had to be done. He deserved to hear it first from you."

Jenny remained silent as tears cascaded down her cheeks.

"Do you need me to come get you? Where are you?"

"No, I'll be fine. I'm just a block away from my pl... Ryan's apartment," she answered listlessly.

"Do you want to meet somewhere?"

"I think I need some time alone. I'll call when I'm ready."

"Whatever you need, Jenny, just know I'll be waiting for your call."

She was glad Dan wasn't pushing himself on her or treating her like a breakable doll. She sat in her car replaying the last six months. The innocent trip up to the cabin, the blizzard... Dan's seduction of her. The realization she loved him. Ryan's eventual acceptance and the threesome that formed from that mutual love. *Why couldn't it last?*

Kelly.

Why did Kelly have to ruin it all? What did she gain by driving them apart? Revenge, sure... but what benefit was that to her? Was there comfort in knowing that Ryan was hurting as much as she'd been hurt? How shallow and cruel of the bitch. Ryan hadn't done anything wrong. It seemed odd that Jenny had been friends with her for years and not been aware of the heartless creature underneath that energetic personality.

Jenny wiped away the tears and drove to a cheap hotel near her work. Until she knew what she was doing, she needed a place to stay—where didn't matter. She lay down on the hard bed and stared up at the ceiling. She was getting married to Dan. The reality of it was slowly sinking in and helped to soften the blow. She dug out her phone and called him. "If you want to meet me over at the Continental, I'm in room 142."

"Excellent. I'll be there soon."

She waited impatiently for his arrival, needing to feel Dan's arms around her. She rushed to the door when he knocked, swinging the door wide open.

Her relief was short-lived. "What are you doing here?"

"I just heard, but I had to hear it from the whore's mouth."

Jenny tried to slam the door shut, but Kelly pushed her way inside. "Oh no, you are not getting rid of me that easy, ho. You are going to have to face me."

Jenny backed away from her, grabbing her cell phone.

"Are you really such a coward? Are you calling Dan to come to the rescue?" she asked in a patronizing tone. "That would be perfect."

Jenny put the phone down. "I am not a coward."

"You are a lot of things, Jen. Cunt, backstabber, bitch, cheater, whore... the list goes on. Fucking two men at the same time? My God! But no, that wasn't enough for you, was it? You have to stab Ryan and me in the heart by marrying *my* man."

"You lost Dan all on your own, Kelly. He pursued me, it wasn't the other way around."

"I know what happened up in the cabin. You fucking spread your legs and begged him. I can just imagine it. You couldn't keep your hands off my boy toy when the opportunity presented itself. All this time I thought we were friends. I was *so* wrong!"

Jenny's eyes narrowed. "You've got that right."

Kelly delivered a hard slap to her cheek. "Don't turn this on me, whore. I didn't make moves on your boyfriend."

Jenny rubbed her stinging skin. "Yeah, but you twisted Ryan's mind to your way of thinking. We were happy together but you just couldn't let that happen."

"Of course! What you were doing was an abomination. You think I was going to sit by and let that continue under my nose?"

"It was none of your business. You broke it off with Dan. You gave up your rights to him."

"I dropped him because I didn't want what you defiled. He was dead to me the moment he touched you. Just as you are dead to me."

"Is that why you tried to drive me off the road? You're fucking insane, Kelly!"

Kelly rushed her, grabbing a fist of Jenny's long hair. "Don't ever call me crazy, you cunt!" Jenny struggled out from under Kelly's grasp, kneeing her soundly in the gut.

"Stay away from me. From all of us!" Jenny screamed.

Kelly cradled her stomach, hissing, "I will make you pay." She started backing towards the door. "You are not marrying Dan, you fucking whore. I promise you that."

"Nothing you can do will stop us from getting married. Nothing!"

Kelly suddenly was back in her face. "Wanna bet?" She cackled like an old woman on her way out of the hotel room, leaving the door open.

Jenny wilted onto the bed, shaken by the confrontation. She literally screeched when she saw a figure at the door. Dan ran into the room, demanding, "What happened?"

"Kelly."

"How did she find you here?"

Jenny shook her head. "I don't know, Dan... Ryan must have called her after I told him our plans. But," she felt a sickening knot building in her stomach, "she must have been there. She must have followed me from his place."

Dan enfolded her in his protective embrace. "We have to file a restraining order."

"Okay," she agreed weakly.

Dan stroked her hair, murmuring over and over again, "I am so sorry, Jenny."

"I didn't get it. I didn't understand how truly nuts she is."

Dan guided her to his car and drove her to the police station. Jenny was fine with their decision to bring the police into it until she saw the officer who had humiliated her twice before.

"You," the man said disdainfully.

Jenny turned around and immediately exited the building. "What good will it do anyway, Dan? A restraining order won't prevent her from getting to me if she's determined."

Dan prodded her back into the police station, insisting on a different officer. The new guy took down her complaint and had her fill out the required paperwork. "Expect to hear within two days," he said before handing her copies of the paperwork. Jenny left the station not feeling an ounce better.

"You are coming with me, Jenny. I already talked to my friend, John. His place is excruciatingly small, but Kelly can't bother you there. The complex has a guard at the door. I don't want you to worry about being alone until this situation is resolved with Kelly."

She was surprised at the relief she felt. A cramped place with others close by would make her feel safe. "That sounds good."

"It'll help me worry less."

Jenny looked up at him sadly. "Dan, I can't believe Ryan told her."

"I don't believe for one second he thought he was placing you in danger. She probably has him convinced she only wants the best for you two."

"Ryan is blind."

"I'll talk to him, Jenny."

She shook her head vigorously. "He won't listen to you, Dan. He blames you for everything."

"Then I will leave him a message at work. Ryan

needs to understand his interaction with her has serious consequences for you."

"Do you think he even cares?" Jenny asked, remembering his rage and anguish.

Dan caressed her cheek lightly. "As hurt as he is, he still loves you, Jenny. He would never willingly cause you harm."

The tears started again. "If you could have seen him today…."

Dan sighed. "Understand, if the situation had been reversed I would have been hurt, but I would still want what's best for you. With time, Ryan will accept your decision. It is better to be upfront now than to drag it out in an attempt to make it easier, because it won't." She buried her face in his chest. "We will get through this, Jenny. It'll be okay."

She wondered if he was saying it to convince himself as much as her.

They headed to his friend's place after picking up her car at the hotel. It turned out that John only had a one-bedroom apartment consisting of a small living room, the single bedroom, and a tiny galley-like kitchen. It was doable for one person, but nearly impossible for three.

Jenny looked the place over and smiled hesitantly at John. "I can't impose like this."

He grabbed a pizza slice out of his fridge and started munching on it. "Not a problem. I spend the majority of my time in my bedroom anyway. You and Dan can sleep on the couch. It's fine. Really the only problem will be the bathroom." He gave Jenny a sideways glance. "I hope you aren't one of those prissy girls who spend hours primping."

Dan wrapped his arms around her and put his chin on top of her head. "No, Jenny is a natural beauty. Primping is not required."

She looked up at Dan, basking in his nearness. "True. I can shower and be out of the bathroom in fifteen minutes, no problem."

John grinned broadly. "Then I think we're in business."

Jenny looked at the small couch. It was going to be cramped, but she was warming to the idea of sleeping nestled in Dan's arms.

"Can you cook?" John asked.

"Probably as well as you," she quipped, "but I'm willing to take on the cooking duties as payment for your kindness."

"Cool." He grabbed another slice of cold pizza and headed to his room. "See you guys later." Just before he shut the door he added, "And don't do anything I wouldn't do."

Jenny glanced over at Dan and grinned. *Like there's any room to get in trouble here.* "Don't worry. We'll behave."

Once the door shut, Dan moved up behind her and growled, "I wouldn't be so sure of that." She sighed in contentment when she felt his warm lips on her neck. Her body melded into his willingly. "I want to take you to see my parents tomorrow after work."

Jenny stiffened and moved out of his embrace.

"Do they know?"

"Not yet. That's the reason for the visit, my little kumquat." Dan gathered her back in his arms and nibbled on her ear.

Jenny couldn't appreciate his attempt at seduction as nausea settled in. "How do you think they will take the news? It'll be strange for them, don't you think?" Jenny knew that Dan's parents had really liked Kelly and had taken Dan's breakup hard.

"Don't worry, baby. They will happy for us. How could they not be? We are meant for each other. It's carved in the tree."

She smiled at the memory of his proposal and kissed his warm lips for reassurance. "I love you."

He picked her up and twirled her around the cramped space. "Love you more, woman."

Interference

Dan met her after work the following evening and they made the hour and a half drive to his parents' house. Mr. and Mrs. Hayes lived on the opposite side of the city, backing up to the foothills. Although Jenny had been to their place on several occasions, it felt like the first time to her. "This is going to go bad. I can feel it," she told him as she got out of the car.

"Jenny, it's just my parents. I don't know why you're so nervous."

She tried to smile, but she could not rid herself of the growing pit in her stomach. "Well, at least it'll be good to get it over with."

Dan held up her left hand and caressed her ring finger. "This is more than just a courtesy call. I plan to ask for my great-grandmother's ring."

"Oh, Dan!" Jenny loved the idea of wearing a part of his family's history. It would mean so much because the ring was a symbol of the same couple who'd built the cabin. "That would be incredible."

"I'm glad you think so." He kissed her hand before he rang the doorbell. From deep inside the house she heard his father shout, "Come in!"

The foyer was elegant, full of expensive sculptures. Jenny had always liked Mrs. Hayes' taste in art. "Mom and Dad, Jenny's here with me."

Both adults walked into the entrance hall with shocked expressions. "Jenny?" his mother repeated.

Dan wrapped his arm around Jenny and smiled confidently. "Yes, I want you to meet my future wife." Jenny's eyes widened. He hadn't wasted a second.

Mrs. Hayes frowned and turned to her husband. They stared at each other without saying anything.

"It's a pleasure to see you both again," Jenny offered, wanting to kill the awkward silence.

His father recovered first. "We're glad you could come."

Dan shook his head. "What's up with you guys? I just introduced my future wife to you. Don't you have anything more to say?"

Mrs. Hayes finally spoke. "It's a mistake."

Jenny's heart contracted in pain. She turned to Dan and then tried to make a break for it, but he held her tight.

"There's no mistake. I proposed to her under the same tree you did twenty years ago." He looked down at Jenny with his devastating brown eyes. "I was lucky she said yes."

"It's not right," Mrs. Hayes insisted.

"Now come on, Harriet. Let's invite them in and sit down to a meal like civilized people."

Dan snorted. "What's going on here?"

"You should know that Kelly called and explained what's been going on between the two of you," Mrs. Hayes replied. She looked at Jenny with disdain. "It's not right, young lady."

Dan pulled Jenny to him protectively. "Don't talk to my fiancée that way, Mother."

Mr. Hayes took control of the situation. "Let's walk into the dining room and sit down. Dinner's on the table and we can discuss this like the reasonable people we are."

When Mrs. Hayes protested, he grabbed her arm and forced her to follow him down the hallway. Jenny seethed inside. Kelly was on a warpath where nothing was sacred.

They spent an uncomfortable dinner discussing mundane things instead of the elephant in the room. Once dessert was served, Dan cut to the chase. "Look, the reason I came with Jenny tonight is to let you know of our wedding plans and to get Gammy's ring."

Mrs. Hayes visibly tensed. "You can't have it."

"Mom, you can't be serious," Dan objected.

"No harlot is going to wear Gammy's ring. It's not right!"

Mr. Hayes put his hand on his wife's shoulder and squeezed. "We are not going to debase ourselves by calling people names, Harriet." He looked at Dan and said, "We are opposed to the lifestyle you have chosen. We are not comfortable with it and cannot condone it, son."

Dan said defensively, "What lifestyle? Jenny and I are going to get married just like the two of you. I don't see the problem here."

Mr. Hayes cleared his throat. "We know about the threesome. Frankly, I find it disgusting."

Mrs. Hayes whimpered as if the mere thought of it harmed her in some way.

Jenny was proud of Dan. There wasn't a moment of hesitation when he answered, "What Ryan, Jenny and I chose to do as grown adults has no bearing on you. However, things have changed recently and Jenny and I are getting married. I would like the ring Gammy promised I could give to my wife."

"You can't have it!" Mrs. Hayes snapped.

Mr. Hayes patted her shoulder to quiet her. "Son, are you telling me that you plan to have a traditional marriage… no extra partners involved?"

"Yes, Father."

Mr. Hayes sat back in his chair, digesting the news while Mrs. Hayes stared daggers at Jenny.

"Mother, stop it. This is your future daughter-in-law and the woman I love. You will treat her with the same love and respect you give me."

Mrs. Hayes huffed and jerked her head away angrily.

His father let out a long sigh before speaking. "Gammy specifically gave you the ring. Whether we agree with your choice or not, I do not see how we can deny her wishes." With that, he got up and left the room with Mrs. Hayes trailing behind him, protesting loudly.

Jenny tried to leave again, but Dan grasped her hand and said smoothly, "Don't run scared, Jenny. You and I know this is right. Give them time to adjust."

"But Dan, they know everything." Jenny buried her face in her hands. "They know about the ménage."

"While I admit it is disconcerting to have my parents know intimate details about our sex life, what does it matter? We are adults and have nothing to be ashamed of."

Somehow, Dan made the awkward situation manageable and she appreciated the way he handled his mother. He remained respectful without compromising himself or Jenny.

"Even though I want to run away, I will stay with you," she said with determination. Dan leaned over and gave her a gentle, lingering kiss.

"Must you?" Mrs. Hayes complained as they reentered the room.

Jenny noticed that Mr. Hayes held a small wooden box. He hesitated for a moment before handing it to Dan. "Are you sure, son? You wanted to marry Kelly once." He looked at Jenny and said, "I'm sorry to ask this in front of you." Then he turned back to Dan. "Are you positive Jenny is the one you want to spend the rest of your life with, especially given her sordid past?"

Dan asked coolly, "What sordid past?"

Mrs. Hayes piped up, "She enticed you to join in that unnatural lifestyle."

"Actually, that was Ryan's idea. Of the three of us, Jenny is the one who was enticed, Mother."

"What's wrong with you? Why would my son need to fuck another man?" Mrs. Hayes cried.

Dan clenched his jaw as he stood up from the table. "You have been listening to that vindictive bitch. Kelly has no idea what happened between us, but I can assure you it did not involve homosexual acts. Even if it had, what business is it of it yours, Mother? I *am* a grown man." He looked at both of his parents. "Kelly assumed you were fools. I am shocked you played into her hands so easily."

Mrs. Hayes turned purple. "Kelly is a dear. How dare you try to make her out as some kind of monster! I love that girl. I could never love this"—she pointed at Jenny—"jezebel."

"Now, now, Harriet. Let's not say anything we'll regret," Dan's father said evenly.

Jenny had enough. "I am not a whore, Mrs. Hayes. I love your son. I love him more than life itself. I was honored when he asked me to marry him under the same tree that Mr. Hayes proposed to you under. I felt honored to become a part of this distinguished family, but I will not be insulted. You are mistaken about Kelly, but unlike her, I will not throw around insults."

Jenny got up to leave, but Dan gracefully took her arm and walked her out, announcing behind him, "And that's why I love this woman." Jenny had never felt that powerful before as she headed to the front door. She knew with certainty that nothing was going to stop their marriage. Kelly's worst had just been a bump in the road. *Nothing to worry about.*

"Son," Mr. Hayes called out. "Don't forget this." He walked over and handed Dan the small box.

"Thanks, Dad." Mr. Hayes opened his arms and the two hugged. It warmed Jenny's heart to see it. He then gazed kindly at Jenny. "Welcome to our family." He put his large arms around her small frame and gave her a stiff hug. Although it wasn't full of the warmth he'd given his son, Jenny appreciated the token gesture.

"Thank you, Mr. Hayes."

"Dad to you soon," he said.

"Oh God, do you have to say that?" Mrs. Hayes complained from the hallway.

"Get used to it, Harriet. You know our son. Once his mind is set, nothing can stop him."

Jenny glanced at Mrs. Hayes and saw her lips pursed in an ugly frown. "Good-bye, Mrs. Hayes." Jenny *almost* said 'Mother' but figured that would be pushing it. Although she would have enjoyed being friends with Dan's mom, having at least one member of his family accept her was enough.

They left the house and headed to the car in silence. Once inside, Dan announced, "I want to take you somewhere, but it means a late night for us."

She shrugged her shoulders. "Not like we are

going to get any sleep on that tiny couch."

"Excellent." When he turned towards the mountains, she knew exactly where he was headed. Jenny smiled and leaned her head on his shoulder.

They made it to the cabin after eleven. The area was bathed in the eerie glow of a full moon, giving it an otherworldly appearance. Dan got out of the car first, insisting on opening the door for Jenny. "Now I can do this properly, the way I wanted to."

Jenny gasped at how cold it was and wrapped her arms around herself.

Dan walked her under the shadow of the pine tree and got down on one knee amongst the snow. He opened the small wooden box and took out the ring. Jenny saw the glint of its diamond in the moonlight. With white vapors escaping with each word he asked, "Jenny Marie Cole, would you consent to be my wife?"

Her smile was so wide it hurt. "Yes, Dan, I more than consent. I am *happy* to be your wife."

Dan took her hand in his and slid the ring on her finger. She giggled with joy when he stood up and pulled her to his chest. "You make me a very happy man, Miss Cole," Dan said, picking her up and heading towards the cabin.

"No, Dan."

He stopped in his tracks. "What do you mean 'no'?"

Jenny saw visions of Mrs. Hayes standing in the doorway and it killed any feeling of passion. "I don't want to do it here. Not in your family's cabin. At least not until your mom accepts me."

He set her back down on the ground. "Don't let her change anything between us."

She looked up at Dan and smiled. "Nothing can change how I feel about you, but I don't feel comfortable here." She headed back to the car and tilted her head when she looked back at him. "So, now what are you going to do?"

He moved up behind her, growling in her ear, "I believe I'm going to have to get a little creative with you."

Jenny shivered in delight. "I happen to like the sound of that."

He smiled mischievously as he walked around to the driver's side. "Damn, Jenny, you're in for a ride now."

"I can't wait!" Jenny looked down at her hand with the diamond winking back at her playfully. *A lifetime of this…*

Dan did not head back to the city; instead he made a left at the crossroads heading further into the mountains.

"Where are we going, Dan?"

"Trust me."

After twenty minutes on a bumpy road they came up to a large pond surrounded by snow-covered pine trees. The moon shone brightly on the icy pond. It was spectacular and serene.

"This place is breathtaking."

"My secret spot, baby. Haven't shared it with anyone before." He leaned over and kissed her on the lips. "A perfect place to take my fiancée."

He got out of the car and motioned her to follow. The two stood before the small mountain lake and drank in its pristine beauty despite the bitter cold. Dan snuck a hand around her and pulled her to him. "Will this do, future Mrs. Hayes?"

"What? Here? On the snowy ground? You on the bottom, buddy!"

He chuckled. "Not on the ground, my love. On the hood of the car under the stars, in the presence of God's glorious creation."

"But it's freezing!"

"True, but the hood won't be." Dan walked to the back of the car and pulled out a blanket from the trunk. He unfolded the large fleece and laid it over the hood.

Despite the covering, Jenny shivered. The thought of her naked skin being exposed to the harsh winter air was not sexy. "I don't know, Dan…"

"What? Are you chickening out on me?" he scoffed.

Dan used the "chicken" word. He *knew* what that did to her. "No, I am not chickening out." Jenny started unbuttoning her shirt as proof.

"That's more like it," he encouraged, stripping off his own shirt.

The two walked over to the car and Dan helped her sit on the edge of the hood. His hands caressed her shoulders and then snuck behind her back. She felt him unhook her bra and it fell away from her breasts. The chilly air had an immediate effect on her nipples. "Oh, lovelies," Dan growled, "have you missed me?" His warm lips encased one breast while his fingers tugged and teased the other.

Jenny threw her head back, bracing herself against the car with her elbows. "They have missed you, Dan. Very much…"

He pushed her down as he kissed his way up to her collarbone. She resisted, but Dan was insistent in his pressure and she gasped when she finally gave in and felt the warmth of the blanket. "Oh, now that is nice," she purred.

She relaxed on the hood and did not resist when Dan pulled at her jeans. He removed her panties next and let them fall to the snowy ground. Then Dan spread her legs open so that he could admire her femininity. She found the bitter cold on her clit sexy.

"You are perfection, Jenny. Your Cherokee skin, that dark little mound, those pink inviting lips…" He bent down and took a long, hot lick of her sex. "There is nothing as perfect as you."

"You, Dan," she whispered.

He shook his head. "No, my love. I am your complement, but you are the prize."

Jenny was touched by his words and wanted him inside her that instant. Jenny wiggled seductively on the car. "Partake of me, complement."

She giggled as Dan awkwardly stripped out of the rest of his clothes. He crawled onto the hood, lying on top of her. Her giggles instantly quieted when his shaft pressed against her opening. "Dan…"

"Yes?" he asked, remaining completely still.

"I need you."

He pressed his cock harder against her inner lips. "Is this what you need, woman?"

She nodded, smiling up at him. Dan slowly pushed the head of his shaft inside her warm depths—and then stopped. He leaned over and kissed her. His cold lips pressed hard against hers, creating a fire in her core. Her inner muscles squeezed his shaft and he growled in appreciation. He inched a little further in.

Jenny cried, "More of you…"

His white smile glowed in the moonlight. "More? You are at my mercy, my love." He pulled out and rested his shaft against her swollen lips.

"No! Please…" she whimpered.

He chuckled and reentered her, his shaft already cold from the momentary exposure to the air. "You are too hot for me to resist." He thrust hard and Jenny arched her back in response, wanting his full length. He placed his hands on either side of her and began sliding in and out rhythmically in a slow controlled manner, his cock igniting the fire even further.

Her nipples ached in tight constriction while her loins coated her lover in her dripping adoration. She looked up at Dan, the moon a halo around his face. "I love you, fiancé."

He groaned and possessed her then. Dan enclosed her delicate wrists with his strong hands as his lips commanded her mouth and his cock released its passion. She moaned, rejoicing in the repeated thrusts of his masculine ownership. He knew her body, knew how to make her combust in unquenchable lust.

"Baby…" he breathed just before his body tensed and his eyes closed in rapture. Jenny concentrated all of her focus on his shaft as it shuddered, cherishing his orgasm. She lay there panting afterwards, content with the weight of his body pressing down on her.

Jenny assumed their session was over but Dan slowly stroked her with his spent shaft, rubbing that area he knew so well. She felt the tension rise and the fire ignite into a growing inferno. There was no stopping the surge that crashed over her and stole her breath away. Her body milked his cock with its rhythmic tightening. The fact he was no longer hard made her orgasm that much more intense as she felt the fullness of each contraction. This time she was the one shuddering afterwards.

"Baby, baby," he whispered in her ear.

She wrapped her legs around him. "I love you, Dan. You'll never know how much."

They lay in the freezing mountain air, lost in the afterglow. They were a couple now, exclusive lovers. It was an incredible feeling, incredible except for the harsh chill creeping into her bones…

"Dan," she said, struggling underneath.

He smiled down at her, not moving. "Yes?"

"I'm getting cold."

"Are you, my love?"

She struggled harder and was met by his chuckles as he pressed her against the hood with his body weight. She growled playfully, certain she could topple him off the car. She twisted and squirmed, but when that didn't work she tried to tickle him. He easily captured her arms and held them back down. She was utterly defenseless. "Dan!"

His laughter filled the forest. "What, my little kumquat?"

"Get off me," she commanded.

"But I like having you at my mercy," he purred into her ear.

She struggled unsuccessfully and was about to complain again when his lips met hers, taking all resistance away. She became acutely aware that his cock had recovered and was pressing against her thigh. "Oh…"

"See what you do?" He slipped back into her seamlessly and began pumping her a second time. Having just come, her body was immediately responsive and throbbed in time with his thrusts.

Dan pulled himself up. "Your breasts are so big and luscious, woman." He cupped them in each hand and then braced himself against them as he slowly pulled out and pushed back in forcefully.

Jenny stretched her arm up, touching the windshield with her fingertips. She looked up at the few stars bright enough to compete with the moon as he took her again. The feeling of being held down by his large hands pressing against her breasts added a raw element she hadn't experienced before. She thrilled at the feeling of possession. *I am Dan's.*

His thrusts were more pronounced this second time—deeper, demanding and hard. "You... feel... so... good," he panted in time with each stroke.

She panted with him, her body building up to a dangerous level, so intense it felt as if it might rip her apart. The freezing temperatures no longer mattered as her body tensed for a massive orgasm. Her hips thrust up violently and Dan's cock met her perfectly. They both cried out as her body convulsed in a powerful explosion. Jenny strained against his strong hands while he held her in place as the orgasm claimed her. She screamed into the night, alerting all the wildlife to her climax.

"That's it, baby," Dan said lustfully.

It seemed to go on forever, and somehow he maintained control until after her last contraction ended. Then he gritted his teeth and pumped her slowly, letting his shaft fill her with his seed. He collapsed on her then and she wrapped her arms around him.

"How do you do it?"

"What?"

"Share new facets of yourself each time?"

He lifted his head and brushed back his hair all sexy-like. "You are my muse, I am continually inspired." Dan gave her a ghostly white smile and helped her off the hood. They dressed in a rush and piled back into the car, shivering from the cold.

Dan turned the heat on full blast. Once Jenny stopped shaking, she drifted off to sleep. But she woke with a start when the car jerked.

"What happened?"

Dan turned off the heat and unrolled his window, letting wind whip around the car. "Remind me never to have mind-blowing sex just before a long drive in the dark."

"You fell asleep?"

"Nodded off for a second, but that's all it takes." He turned towards her. "Mind if you keep me company the rest of the drive down?"

Jenny unrolled hers as well to rid herself of the need to sleep. Even with the cold blast of air on her face, all she wanted to do was close her eyes. To keep herself awake, she found her favorite station and turned up the radio. At one point, she saw his eyes flutter shut. "Dan, wake up!"

His head jerked back up and his eyes popped open. Dan slapped his face a couple of times before turning to her. "Thanks. I won't let that happen again."

He leaned forward and spent the rest of the long, difficult drive with his eyes glued to the road. Both of them were exhausted by the time they finally made it to John's place. They made their way to the couch and curled up together, falling asleep in their clothes.

Jenny woke up to, "Hey, Sleepyhead!" She cracked open an eye and saw John staring at Dan.

He tilted his head and asked, "Could you wake

him?"

Jenny wiggled against Dan until he began to stir. John told him, "That Ryan guy stopped by last night wanting to talk to you. Just thought you should know." He picked up his keys and turned back to them. "By the way, it's almost eight. You're late."

Both Jenny and Dan rolled off the couch. She looked at his rumpled hair and laughed, knowing she must look as unkempt. "I don't have time to change. Think anyone will notice?"

"If they do, I'm sure they'll have a good idea why and feel only jealousy."

"Good."

As the two headed out the door Dan said, "I think I'll visit Ryan after work. See what he wanted last night."

"Okay… I hope it goes well," she said with trepidation.

"I'm not worried. Ryan has every right to confront me. We both need to square things."

The day went smoothly with only one person commenting on her clothing. Lucky for her, it was a slow day of trading. Jenny stopped by the grocery store after work and picked up items for lasagna. Knowing that Dan would be gone for a couple of hours, she decided to take the time to create a nice, hearty meal. John came out of his room and patted her on the back when he saw what she was making.

"Hot damn, I love having a woman in the house." With that, he disappeared into his bedroom again and shut the door with no offer to help.

Typical man.

Jenny had just topped the noodles with fresh mozzarella and was stuffing it into the oven when Dan appeared at the door.

Her hand flew to her mouth the instant she saw him. "Oh my God, what did he do?" She ran across the small apartment, focused on his red, swollen eye.

"Ryan sucker-punched me. Didn't see it coming."

She shook her head in disbelief. "Rye did this?" She tried to caress the tender area, but Dan grabbed her hand and kissed it before putting it back at her side.

"Yeah, Ryan was seething with rage. It is a side of him I have never seen before, but... I can't blame him." He walked over to the couch and sat down, laying his head back. "Fuck, that was nuts."

Jenny grabbed a bag of peas out of the freezer and sat next to him, gently placing it over his eye. He opened his one good eye and smiled sadly. "Thanks."

"What happened, Dan?"

He groaned and shut his eyes again, remaining silent for several moments. "Ryan is pretty torn up. I thought he wanted to talk, but really all he wanted was to punch the shit out of me. He got one good hit in before I could defend myself."

"Does he look as bad?" Jenny asked, worried for both men.

Dan snorted. "No, I held him down until he didn't have any fight left."

She couldn't hide her disbelief. "How is that possible? Ryan is no shrinking violet."

"I have an arm hold that immobilizes even the strongest man, although I'm sure he will be sore in the morning. After Ryan stopped threatening to kill me, we talked or at least tried to."

She asked quietly, "What did he say?"

Dan looked nauseous when he answered her. "Jenny… he cried. I have never seen Ryan…" He turned away from her. He muttered, "He's struggling."

She shrank away from Dan. It felt wrong that they were so happy while Rye was suffering so profoundly. "Tell me exactly what happened."

"He blames me for everything like you said, and is convinced we were having an affair long before the cabin. Ryan claims we've played him for a fool. But it is not just that." He looked at her in concern. "His work is going badly. His assistant quit and he has a new temp who doesn't know what she is doing. It's affecting his productivity and possibly costing him the Jr. Partnership. He's got nothing left, baby. He looks… terrible."

She knotted her hands in worry. "What are we going to do?"

"There is nothing we can do. You and I continue forward with our plans. Whether we go through with our marriage or not, Ryan will hurt the same." He stroked her cheek. "It is the loss of you that he is mourning most."

"I feel so awful, Dan."

He took the bag of peas off his eye and said with conviction, "If you and I weren't so right, I would question our actions. However, I have never felt such certainty before. We are meant for each other. I will not allow anyone or anything to tear us apart."

"Even when it crushes your best friend?" she whispered.

Dan winced but answered, "Even then."

Jenny cuddled up to him, laying her head on his shoulder. She whimpered softly, "Are we going to hell for this?"

"No, time will prove us right. We just have to get through this part. It's like birth; it squeezes like a motherfucker, but then you see the light and breathe in life-sustaining air."

Vendetta

That night, Jenny was desperate for connection with Dan. She needed to feel his comfort and physical contact. She lay beside him on the couch resentful that they could not be intimate.

"What's wrong, Jenny?"

She whispered, "I need you."

He held her closer and kissed her, but it was not enough to ease the ache in her soul. "I need you, Dan, but it's not possible." She looked in the direction of John's door. The light was still on and she could hear him talking to himself.

"I'm sure I can oblige you, my love." Dan's fingers slipped under her long pajama shirt.

She stopped him. "We can't! I don't want John to come out and catch us. Just the thought of it gives me chills."

He murmured in her ear, "Chills can be a good thing." His hand returned to its task, lifting the hem of the shirt higher and disappearing between her legs. Jenny closed her eyes, wanting him to continue despite her qualms. She started grinding against his hand, marking his fingers with her wet excitement. His finger slipped into her opening and she let out only the barest of gasps.

Dan pulled down his sleeping trunks. Her loins tingled in anticipation as he tugged at her panties. She was hesitant, but unwilling to stop him because she *needed* to feel his shaft inside her. She stifled her cry when the round head of his cock pressed against her outer lips. She opened her legs slightly to allow better access. Dan pressed harder and his shaft slipped into her just as John opened his door. Dan became stock still.

They watched John head towards the kitchen without looking at them. Dan adjusted the blanket, but didn't pull out. Jenny's heart beat rapidly as she lay there.

John grabbed the pan of lasagna from the fridge and cut a large piece, placing it in the microwave and hitting the power button. He looked over at Jenny. "I can't resist good Italian food. Damn thing has been calling to me for hours."

Dan grumbled, "But you already had two pieces not that long ago."

"Doesn't matter. I'm like a camel. I must fill up to capacity." John eyed the piece hungrily as it spun behind the glass.

They both watched John take the plate from the microwave after the beep and then sit down at the table to eat it.

Jenny groaned inside. Dan's hand traveled to her stomach as he readjusted and pushed his cock in deeper while asking John, "You sure you don't want to eat that in your room?"

John looked up. "Sorry, man, I can't stand having food in my bedroom. I'll try to eat fast, but I heated it up too much. The cheese is burning my tongue."

Jenny wiggled her ass against Dan while telling John, "Don't feel you have to rush. No need to burn your mouth on our account." She laid her head down as if she was going back to sleep.

Dan moved centimeters only, thrusting imperceptibly in and out. Every nerve ending in her body was focused on his incremental movements. She resettled, helping his shaft to penetrate more deeply.

This connection was what she needed, what she had been impatient for after Dan's revelation about Ryan and his assurance they were meant to be together no matter the cost. Being connected again, she was in agreement. They were two people who were made for each other, like Romeo and Juliet. No matter the cost, no matter the consequences, their love could not be denied.

Dan laid his head next to her head and breathed warmth into her ear. "I love you," he whispered as he continued stroking her a centimeter at a time.

She heard John blowing on his meal, smacking his lips, trying to eat quickly so they could 'sleep'. He had no idea what he had stumbled into. There was a sense of wicked fun, making love in front of another without the person's knowledge. Jenny readjusted again, hoping she wasn't being too obvious. Dan groaned a little too loudly, causing John to look up at them.

"I am hurrying as fast as I can, man. It is not my fault Jenny makes a killer lasagna for a Cherokee."

"Mom was Italian," she sighed longingly.

Dan shook his head at John and grasped her hips, concentrating the head of his cock on that spot he knew so well. The incremental movements began to have their effect. Jenny felt her nipples hardening, her heart pounding in her chest from his effort. She struggled not to move as the rhythmic pulses began.

She lost connection to everything but the feeling of Dan inside her. Jenny held her breath as wave after delicious wave washed through her. When her body finally relaxed she felt Dan stiffen as his essence permeated her being. She forgot herself and moaned softly.

"Okay, okay! I'll leave. You don't have to be so dramatic, Jenny." She heard John throw his plate in the sink before heading to his bedroom and shutting the door.

Dan chuckled in her ear. "Yes, my dear, don't be so dramatic when you come."

She turned her head towards him. "You are a bad man, Dan Hayes, a very bad man. If John only knew he would kick us both out."

"That… or he would ask to watch."

She buried her head in her pillow and giggled. But a random thought of Ryan surprised her and she fell silent.

"It'll be okay," Dan said, pulling her closer. "We will all make it through."

Jenny held onto those words the next morning. On her drive to work, she kept seeing visions of Ryan with tears in his eyes holding his hand out to her. It weighed so heavily on her soul that by the time she got to work, her stomach was in knots.

The moment she entered the office, she knew something was off. The place suddenly got quiet and every eye turned to her. She looked around nervously and giggled like an idiot. No one said a thing. She felt the fight-or-flight instinct take over, but she willed herself to walk to her desk and sit down. On her keyboard was a picture. She was kissing Dan while Ryan looked at her lustfully, his hands on her breasts. In large red letters across the bottom it read, *Whore!*

Jenny scanned the office and noticed the same picture scattered throughout the office. It seemed Kelly had left one on every desk. She had no idea how Kelly had gotten such an intimate shot of the three of them, but it ripped at her heart to have everyone looking at it—at her. She tore the picture into pieces and tossed them in the trash, trying not to show the panic creeping into her heart.

"Miss Cole, come into my office," Mr. Thomas commanded.

Jenny got up on unsteady feet and walked to his corner office. She could feel a myriad of judgmental stares piercing her back.

"Sit," he ordered, directing her to a chair across from his desk when she shut the door. "We are a conservative company, Miss Cole. The public expects that we conduct ourselves in a professional manner at all times. Even outside this office." He scowled harshly. "We do not invite scandal."

"I understand, but..." Jenny began.

"I need to know if this photograph is real," he demanded.

She closed her eyes. Jenny was tempted to say it was photoshopped, but when she opened her mouth, she couldn't. "Yes," she answered, the blood rushing to her cheeks.

"You have proven yourself unworthy of our clients' trust. You are terminated as of this moment. Please collect your things and go. We will deal with the details later."

The stern look on his face shamed her. She stood up, needing to grab the back of the chair for support. She turned from him and headed towards the door. "You disgust me," he growled under his breath. The way he said it made her feel filthy and unclean.

Even though she tried to remain courageous, tears fell as she returned to her desk and blindly gathered a few things, cradling them to her chest. Jenny looked ahead of her, concentrating on the door in her attempt to leave without further incident.

A notoriously late employee met Jenny at the door and held it open for her. His smile faltered when he saw her tears. She couldn't take any more and ran to her car, slamming it shut before screaming. "Fuck you! Fuck you, Keeeeellllllly!"

Jenny leaned her head back and forced herself to breathe. She'd just lost her job. Her reputation as a broker was compromised. How could she recover from this?

I can't…

She called Dan, but then couldn't bring herself to tell him what happened. "Never mind, Dan. There is something I've got to do." She hung up and started the car, determined to face her enemy head on. If Kelly thought she was allowed to embarrass Jenny at her work, then it was only fair to return the favor. She consciously kept to the speed limit, not wanting to risk another encounter with the police.

The entire drive Jenny imagined how she would cut Kelly down in front of her coworkers, making her feel the same level of humiliation Jenny felt. There was a sense of exhilaration at the thought.

When she pulled into the parking lot she was shocked to see Dan there. *What the hell?*

He walked up to the car and motioned her to unroll the window. Jenny did so reluctantly. "I had a feeling this was where you were headed."

"What? She called you to gloat?" Jenny spat.

"No, there was something in your voice…" Dan opened the door and pulled her out of the car, enfolding her in a tight embrace. "What happened, baby? Tell me."

Jenny growled, "The bitch littered my office with photos of the three of us. I lost my job, Dan!"

He squeezed her tighter. "I'm so sorry. I can't imagine."

"It was fucking awful and embarrassing!" She felt her anger building. "You can't imagine because it didn't happen to you. Everyone in the office saw it. I was fired on the spot and made to feel like the scum of the earth. I have never felt so low in my life!"

Dan remained silent, which pissed her off. "My reputation is shot, Dan. How the hell am I going to recover from this? My professional life is ruined." She struggled to get out of his arms. "You said this would be worth the consequences, but look at me! I have crushed Ryan's heart, tarnished my reputation and lost my job. How is love worth this? It's not!"

He lifted her chin and looked her in the eye. "Fine. Don't hold back. Tell me how you feel."

"I am so fucking angry right now I could explode! I hurt so badly in here," she cried, pounding her chest, "because I ripped Rye's heart out. I want to die from shame. I felt like a whore today." She looked at Dan accusingly. "I have never felt that way in my life."

He let go of her. "What are you trying to say, Jenny?"

"Maybe *we* aren't worth this. Maybe I've made the biggest mistake of my life."

His gaze was unwavering. "Do you really believe that?"

Dan's face was unreadable as he waited for her answer. She'd lost nearly everything, but looking into his dark brown eyes one fact remained clear—losing Dan would overshadow everything else. "No," she said miserably.

He cupped her cheek and searched her eyes. "I thought I almost lost you just now."

Jenny glanced at Kelly's office building. "She came close to beating me."

"But she didn't and she won't," he said gruffly. He pulled her to him and pressed her cheek into his chest. "Birthing pains, baby. We are almost there."

She closed her eyes and sighed. "Almost there…"

Dan insisted on taking her car, leaving his in the parking lot. He drove her to a swanky hotel cradled in the scenic foothills of the Rockies. She wondered what his plans were, because she felt physically and emotionally spent. He asked her to undress and then followed suit. "Lay on your stomach with your legs spread slightly open, Jenny."

"I'm not in the mood, Dan."

"Yes, you are." He crawled onto her and straddled her ass. Instead of sex, he gave a deep massage. "Relax and let my hands love you."

She completely melted into the bed as his fingers made love to her skin. After he was done with the massage, Dan turned her over and lay beside her, playing gently with her hair. Jenny shuddered in pleasure as tingling chills traveled down her spine.

She opened her eyes and stared at Dan, realizing

it was time to return the favor. "Lie back. Your woman wants to love you the same way."

Dan looked surprised but leaned back and closed his eyes, smiling to himself.

Jenny grazed the toned muscles of his chest with her fingertips. His coarse blond hair contrasted with his smooth muscles. She twirled her finger in a patch of chest hair. "You are a handsome man. I have always thought so. From this manly chest hair," her finger moved to his torso, "to that flat stomach with a cute outtie." His stomach muscles twitched when she lightly circled his belly button. "I even love..." Her fingers trailed downward and she felt him tense, but she continued down his hairy leg to his toes. "These skinny toes." She bent over and kissed his big toe. On a whim, she encased his toe with her lips and sucked lightly.

"You wicked girl."

Her lips made a popping sound when she released the appendage. "I *am* playing unfair." She pulled her body on top of his and lay on him, naked skin against naked skin.

Dan wrapped his arms around her, saying, "I think I know how to solve our problems."

She lifted her head, surprised at the serious look on his face. "Oh yeah?"

He brushed the hair from her eyes. "I think we should get married now."

She asked wearily, "When you say now, what do you mean?"

"Two weeks at the latest."

Jenny shook her head. "What, do you want to go to Vegas?"

He chuckled and her whole body bounced with his laughter. "No, baby. Let's get married in the mountains next to the cabin. I don't need a big wedding, do you?"

She propped herself up on his chest with her arms folded before answering. "Big no... but it's winter, Dan. It'll be freezing up there. I happen to know from personal experience."

He grinned and tweaked her nose. "You can dress in furs to keep warm."

"I detest furs, Dan!"

He laughed. "Fine, no fur. A nice long coat that follows the beauty of your curves." His hands grazed her body, landing on her shapely ass. "What do you think?"

"Are you talking about an outdoor wedding?" she asked incredulously.

"Yes, on the pond. It is completely frozen and won't thaw until spring."

Jenny took a few seconds to let the thought sink in. A wedding on frozen water, near the cabin where it all began. It felt complete, a full circle. "I think it sounds perfect."

He smiled. "Once we are married, Kelly will have to give up and Ryan will be able to move on. It's this limbo that is killing us."

She looked at him despondently. "But I was hoping that Rye would be at our wedding, Dan. There is no way he will come around in two weeks' time."

He pulled her down and kissed her forehead. "You will have to give up on that idea, Jenny. Ryan is hurting too much to give us a gift like that."

"I know," she whispered.

Her heart began to beat wildly when she thought, *We're getting married in two weeks.* "We'd better call our families to get things rolling." She crawled off Dan and fished the cell phone from her purse.

"What? No sex?" Dan complained.

"Nope, trying to pull off a wedding nobody wants is not an easy task. Get cracking, Dan. Tell Mama that her little boy is marrying the indecent Indian next Saturday."

He shook his head with a grin. "Something tells me my mother has finally met her match."

Jenny phoned her parents and was disappointed to hear that her mom was out shopping. It meant she had to share the news with her father and she already knew his response. Despite the fact he had married an Italian girl, he'd always hoped she would find a nice Cherokee boy to settle down with. In fact, his whole family had been pinning their hopes on that pipe dream.

"Jenny, why the rush? I understand you've known Dan for years, but this isn't right."

"Doda," she said sweetly, knowing he loved when she called him that, "I love him as much as you love Mama."

"But child, our people…"

"Love doesn't see color, Doda. You know that better than anyone."

His voiced cracked with emotion. "No one will come, Jenny. Not from my side and certainly not from your mother's."

She laughed into the phone. "I know that! After all, I've never met Mama's parents. I just need you and Mama there. Nobody else matters."

"Are you sure this is what you want?"

"I have never been surer in my life." She looked over at Dan, who was having an intense call. "This is the man I am meant to spend my life with."

There was a pregnant pause before he answered. "It won't be easy, Jenny. Trust me, your mother and I have been through it."

"I saw the strength it took and I am just as strong. Dan and I will survive the disdain. We complement each other, Doda, just like you and Mama." She smiled at her fiancé, who had a sour look on his face. *Must be talking to his mother...*

"We will be there," her father said in his deep guttural tone—that tone always gave her confidence as a child.

"Thank you, Doda. Be sure to pack plenty of warm clothes. The ceremony is going to be held on a pond near Dan's family cabin."

"You'll hear no complaints from me. Nature is the only fitting church."

She put the phone back in her purse, blushing as she realized she'd talked to her father in the nude, just like Dan was doing to his mother. Really, neither of them had any decency.

Why not take it up a notch?

Jenny walked over to Dan and knelt down at his feet. He was shaking his head no when she opened her mouth. "Mother, you don't have to worry about it, you don't have to do a thi—" He grunted as Jenny enveloped the head of his shaft with her mouth and wiggled her tongue around the ridge.

Dan stumbled slightly. "Ah, I was saying that we will take care of ev…"

She caressed his balls lightly as she began to suck.

"What's wrong?" he gasped. Dan regained his composure and answered, "Nothing, Mother. What I meant to say is we'll take care of everything. All that is required of you is to attend. Oh, and can you call Marcuuuusss…" His voice rose in pitch as Jenny swallowed the fullness of his shaft down her throat.

He dropped the cell phone and gathered her hair in his hand, helping to guide her gently. It was the first time he'd taken control and it made her quiver. He groaned quietly as she loved him with her throat.

Jenny could hear his mother's muted cries on the phone. "Dan! Dan, is everything okay? Damn it, Dan, where are you?" Jenny pulled out, took a deep breath and slid his shaft back into her tight throat. He shuddered, letting her know he was close. Jenny lightly caressed his balls again and that simple touch caused a chain reaction. She felt them tighten up as his cock pulsated in her throat, his seed flowing into her. *Such a sexy exchange.*

He pulled out and bent down to kiss her cheek before picking up the phone. "It appears there's a mouse in the apartment. I tried to catch it, but the bugger got away. Yeah, I don't think an exterminator is necessary." He looked down at Jenny and winked. "I think a simple mousetrap will suffice."

His mother went on for another minute before Dan interrupted. "So call Marcus and we will be seeing you at the cabin next Saturday." He hung up before she could protest further, then he shook his finger at her.

"Jenny, that was very naughty."

She looked up at him and smiled coyly. "I couldn't help myself. You were naked and all. Kind of begging for it, if you ask me."

He picked her up and flopped her on the bed before crushing her with his weight. "I think I have created a monster. One that swallows men whole."

She kissed his chin. "You have and now you will have to live with the consequences." Her tone became serious when she asked, "Your mom is obviously not happy, but how does your dad feel?"

"My father is surprised, but agreeable. Really, he is not foolish enough to think he can dictate my life. My mother... well, she still has some learning to do." Dan brushed his hair back out of his eyes and her heart skipped a beat. "What about your parents?"

"My mom was out, so I only talked to my dad.

To be honest, he is worried about our mixed marriage but they will be here. He was hoping I would marry within my race. He doesn't realize that people don't care about mixed marriages anymore, just because he and Mama suffered for it. Thankfully, he has no idea how complicated our situation really is. *That* will be the challenging part for us. The way we started is not fairytale material."

"Well, it is for romance novels."

Jenny rolled her eyes and snorted. "Very funny."

"Lighten up, baby. Sure we will get a few judgmental stares in the beginning, but when people see how perfect we are together they will forget our past. How we started will become a memory and those who hated us will grow to envy us."

She nestled in his arms. "You really think so?"

"Not a doubt in my mind." He lifted himself off her and sat on the bed. "Now, put those hands on the headboard. I think some payback is in order."

Jenny smiled as she placed her hands behind her, but she squeaked when he took her thighs and pushed her feet up to the headboard above her head, next to her hands. She found herself completely helpless and that was when his tongue touched her clit in the most intimate way.

"No, Dan. Stop!" she gasped, struggling to breathe in the awkward position.

"I don't think so," he murmured between her thighs.

"I can barely breathe!"

"Then stop talking." His tongue swirled around

her outer folds and brushed her sensitive clit teasingly. It was gentle and sweet, so Jenny relaxed... until he began the relentless flicking of his tongue. She tried to squirm, but movement wasn't possible. She then resorted to whimpering, but he just chuckled.

"Seriously, I can't breathe, Dan. I think I am going to faint."

"Still talking."

He gave her long, hard licks. They sent jolts of fire to her groin each time he lifted his tongue. "Dan..."

"Give in, baby."

He continued his unyielding offensive, causing her legs to shake uncontrollably. She started panting as the heat in her loins turned to a constant burn.

"I can't!"

"Give in to it."

Jenny closed her eyes and forced herself to stop fighting the burning, tingling sensation consuming her. "Ah... aah..." she whimpered as it blurred her senses and her clit began to contract on his tongue.

He stopped licking and pressed his tongue against her clit so she could ride the wave without distraction. When her orgasm finally ebbed he released her legs and she took a deep breath.

"That wasn't fair," she complained while rubbing his blond hair appreciatively.

He winked and lay back down beside her. "All's fair in love, baby."

Romancing the Details

Dan took Friday off to help her look for a dress. "You know, Dan, it really sucks that Kelly would have been the perfect maid of honor. She's so into fashion and parties," Jenny said, thinking about their last shopping trip together when they'd spent hours upon hours trying on clothes.

"You could still ask her if you want," he answered with a grin.

Jenny elbowed him in the ribs. "Yeah, right. Instead of a maid of honor, I am stuck with you and no one to stand beside me at my wedding."

"Isn't there anyone else?"

"I don't have any other close girlfriends. And unlike you, I don't have a sibling I can use as a stand-in."

"I wasn't planning on asking Marcus to be my best man anyway. I hate asymmetry."

Jenny frowned when they pulled up to the dress

shop. "This is not right, Dan. You're not supposed to see the dress before the wedding. It's against the rules."

He raised an eyebrow and chuckled. "When have we played by the rules?" Dan kissed the top of her head. "I personally never understood why the guy was banned from seeing the wedding dress. Heck, it's supposed to wrap the bride up in a pretty bow for the groom. Why shouldn't he have a say in how his present is dressed?"

She needled a finger in between his ribs. "I am not a present! We're equal partners."

"As such, it only makes sense that you and I pick out your dress and my tux together."

Jenny acquiesced with a grin. "Well, when you put it *that* way it makes sense."

"Of course, my little kumquat. I am the voice of sanity in an insane world."

She was surprised how much fun they had together. Dan took a genuine interest in the gowns. It turned out he did not care for modern dresses that looked like party dresses. No, Dan was more traditional. He preferred lace and buttons, which suited Jenny just fine.

She turned in front of the mirror in a dress that caused a stirring in her spirit. The gown hugged her curves seductively, with a sweetheart bodice covered in lace and a back lined in tiny buttons. The dress also had lace gloves that ran up her arms. The hem of the skirt was flirtatiously uneven, showing of a hint of leg. She twirled in front of Dan, beaming.

The look of admiration in his eyes was priceless. "The one," he said simply.

"Yep, the one!" After a couple more turns in front of the mirror, she took it off and handed it to the assistant. "So how much is the dress?"

The girl searched for the tag and announced, "Six thousand dollars."

Jenny's heart dropped. There was no way she could afford that kind of dress after losing her job. She smiled, trying to hide her disappointment. "Oh well. It seems you and I have expensive tastes."

"I'm sorry, Jenny," he said, getting up and walking over to her. "There was that other one we both liked."

"Yeah... but I didn't love it." She sighed, realizing how immature she was being. "That other dress is fine. How much was it again?" she asked the store keeper.

"Five hundred."

Jenny shrugged her shoulders. "Well, you can't beat that." Jenny was touched that the store keeper put the dress into a protective cover with the same reverence and care as if it had been the more expensive dress. It did Jenny's heart good and made her feel better about the choice.

The two then picked out a stylish black tux with a gold vest and red tie for Dan. "I'll be wearing thermal underwear, so what you see is what you get." He struck a handsome pose for her.

Dan looked devastating in it. "I am one lucky girl," Jenny replied with a happy sigh.

The next order of business was to find the coat that would cover up her dress. On the drive to the boutique Jenny told Dan, "I'm glad we didn't get that other dress. It's going to be covered up by a coat anyway."

Dan gave her a playful sideways glance. "We'll buy the most beautiful coat we can find."

Unlike the dress, finding the coat was easy. Dan noticed it in the window of the store as they walked in and pointed it out to her. The tinkling of a bell announced their arrival as they opened the door to the small boutique. An older man greeted the couple.

"Can I help you?"

Dan immediately asked, "How much is the coat?" pointing to the mannequin in the window.

Jenny looked horrified when she saw the fur.

"That stunning piece is nine hundred and fifty."

"It certainly looks worth that," Dan said encouragingly to Jenny.

She whispered, "It has fur on it."

The gentleman overheard her and grinned. "It's faux fur, Miss. If you feel it, though, I bet you will have a difficult time telling the difference."

Jenny looked at the coat again with fresh eyes. It was white with large pearl buttons up the front. It had a large hood which was rimmed in white faux fur, along with the cuffs and the bottom of the coat. It was romantic in every way. Jenny could see why Dan was set on it, but the price scared her. "That seems like a lot of money."

He put his arm around her waist. "It is a gift from me to you. I want to see you standing beside me in that coat, my love."

Jenny smiled at the thought and turned to the man. "Please, can I try it on?"

Dan helped her into the coat and lovingly buttoned her up. He stood back and whistled.

She snuck a peek in the mirror and caught her breath. It fit her curves seductively and the fur made her look like a frost princess. She liked it every bit as much as the fancy dress. "I'm in love with it!" she said, throwing her arms around Dan and giving him a kiss of appreciation.

"Sold," he told the man when she broke the kiss. The gentleman suggested a pair of white leather boots with similar fur lining that seemed made for the long coat. When Dan saw them on her feet he nodded agreeably. "Box them up as well."

The old man smiled. "Wish all my customers were so easy."

Jenny put her arms around Dan's hips and looked up at him. "When it's right, it's right." With the clothing for the wedding taken care of, Jenny felt deliciously content on the drive home.

"Now for the flowers," Dan announced.

"What, we're doing that today too?" Jenny asked in surprise.

"Hey, woman, I took the day off. I plan on getting everything set up so we don't have to worry about it." Instead of a floral shop, Dan took Jenny to a greenhouse. "I know the owner. She said she would take care of us."

Jenny looked at him doubtfully, but followed him inside. A rotund woman with red cheeks met them at the door. "Dan, you finally came to visit me!" She gave him a big hug and then went straight for Jenny. "And this must be Dan's main squeeze!"

Jenny stiffly accepted her hug, thrown off by the enthusiastic greeting of a stranger. She looked at Dan, raising her eyebrow questioningly.

"Sorry, baby. I didn't tell you that Rose is good friends with my mom."

"The best of friends, Bubba," she said, giving Dan a swat on the ass.

The lady is certainly a character. Jenny's next thought was, *What would she be doing hanging around Dan's mom?* "So you've known Dan's mother for a while?"

"Since college. Oh, the trouble she and I used to get into... you wouldn't believe it. But enough about me. You're here about the flowers. I collected several different kinds for you, so you can decide which works best for your wedding."

Jenny wasn't paying attention. She was lost in her own thoughts. *So, Mrs. Hayes has a wild past, does she? I wonder how wild...*

Dan handed her a book of wedding bouquets. "Rose says she can make any in this book. Check it out and pick your favorite. Whatever you want, Jenny."

Rose pulled out the chair and insisted, "You sit here, dear, while Dan and I look at the potted plants

I picked out."

Dan had envisioned a red carpet lined with flowers on the frozen water. It intrigued Jenny, so she let him have free rein to make his vision a reality while she quietly picked out her perfect bouquet. Thumbing through the pages several times, she finally decided on an unusual nosegay of white gardenias, miniature red roses, accented by a few thin sprigs of pine. It looked wintry and romantic.

Her decision made, she got up and walked over to Rose. "Can you make this?"

The affable woman took the book and smiled at the picture. "Yes, but I will make it even more beautiful."

Jenny smiled gratefully, warming up to the woman who so obviously loved Dan like an aunt, a humorously naughty aunt. "Thank you."

The enthusiastic woman gave her another hug, and this time Jenny returned it fully. Anyone who cared about Dan was instantly a friend to her, and Jenny couldn't help wondering if time spent with Rose would eventually reveal surprising secrets of her soon-to-be mother-in-law.

"So, kids, leave it all up to me. Will you come by to pick it up the day of the wedding or the night before?"

Dan put his hand around her shoulder. "Actually, Rose, I was hoping you would hand-deliver them."

Rose's cheeks turned an even brighter shade of red. "Do you mean it, Danny Boy?"

He chuckled lightly. "Of course. I want my auntie to be there when I marry my soulmate."

It was Jenny's turn to blush. Rose insisted on a three-way hug. "Just you wait, kids. My flowers will blow you away."

"And you're sure you can handle the other thing?" Dan asked her.

Jenny looked at him sideways. "What other thing?"

"My surprise, little kumquat."

Rose's jaw dropped. "Did you just call her kumquat? That was my pet name for you when you were a tiny boy." She winked at Jenny. "He *must* be smitten." Jenny knew with certainty that she would grow to love this woman.

As they headed away from the greenhouse Jenny assumed they were going back to John's apartment, but no. Dan pulled up to a hole-in-the-wall bakery. "Our last stop," he promised when he saw her look of exhaustion.

As much as Jenny liked the idea of shopping for a wedding cake, doing all the wedding errands in one day was grueling and she grumbled as she got out of the car. "Is a cake even necessary, Dan? It's not like we are having a reception or anything."

"Totally necessary," he said, lifting her chin up with his finger. His brown eyes sparkled when he added, "This cake will be only for you and me."

His answer melted her heart. "That's so sweet."

"Just because we are having a small wedding doesn't mean I don't want you to have all the trappings."

The bakery was run by an elderly Asian couple. Dan introduced Jenny to them with an ease as if he'd known them his whole life. "Mr. and Mrs. Tran, I would like you to meet my fiancée, Jenny Cole."

Mr. Tran took her hand warmly and bowed. "It is a pleasure to meet you, Miss Cole."

She bowed back, enchanted by the gesture. "It is a pleasure for me as well."

Mrs. Tran spoke in a small, but sweet voice. "We are honored to make your wedding cake. Thank you."

Jenny smiled and looked at Dan. Everyone was so nice and obviously thought the world of Dan. It made her proud to have such a fine man for a husband.

"Mrs. Tran makes exquisite cakes and Mr. Tran ensures it tastes as good as it looks. The perfect combination," he informed her.

Mrs. Tran twittered and looked down at her feet in embarrassment. It was adorable.

"What size of cake, Mr. Hayes?" the old baker asked.

"Just big enough for the two of us. It is a gift to ourselves." He smiled at Jenny with such tenderness her stomach quivered. "But I want it to look as grand as you can make it. Don't hold back," he instructed Mrs. Tran.

"I will do well by you, Mr. Hayes," she answered.

"That I have no doubt," Dan assured her. "I wouldn't want anyone else to handle such an important detail."

The old woman twittered again. Jenny had to stifle a giggle. The woman was just too darn cute. After the details of the cake were finalized, Dan bought two cupcakes and handed her one. "Take a taste and you'll understand how talented these two are."

The cupcake sported a delicate orchid on top. It seemed a shame to eat it, but Jenny took a bite and purred in delight. The cake was incredibly moist and burst with unusual flavors. She could detect ginger and a hint of star anise. It gave the simple cupcake complexity and depth. She chewed it slowly, savoring the exotic sweetness.

Jenny bowed to Mr. Tran. "I never thought cake could taste like this."

He returned the bow and said humbly, "It is my calling."

"Mr. and Mrs. Tran, I am sorry to eat and run but we must go. I'll be back to pick up the cake Friday after work."

"It will be ready, Mr. Hayes," the little woman said, twittering again for no reason.

Jenny finished her last bite of 'cake heaven' in the car. "This will be the best wedding ever! I can't believe you know so many talented people, Dan."

"My mom used to be a social person, always throwing parties and getting involved in the community. But she's changed over the years... it's scary. The older she gets the more she becomes her mother." He turned to Jenny. "And that is not a good thing."

Although Jenny was surprised by his revelation, she did her best not to show it. Mrs. Hayes appeared to have a lot more to her than Jenny imagined. *The years ahead just might be more interesting as I peel back the layers of this unpleasant woman.* The thought made Jenny happy.

With all the wedding details taken care of, Jenny spent the remaining week looking for a job. Word had spread throughout the local brokerages about her disgrace. Some firms would not take her calls because of the scandal. Thankfully, there were a couple that did and her interviews with them were promising.

It gave Jenny hope that employment might be possible after she was told at one interview, "A person's personal life is just that. At our establishment, we only judge our employees based on their dedication and work ethic. Fail us in that, and we will send you packing." She was informed that they would get in touch with her the following week.

Things were looking up. Kelly's attempts to ruin her had only caused her to grow stronger. Jenny yelled in defiance. "Take that, bitch!"

"What was that?" John asked from his room.

Jenny blushed. "Oh nothing. Just feeling a little feisty today."

"Hey, before you move out, could you make another pan of lasagna?"

"Not a problem. In fact, I will make a whole pan just for you," she called to him.

He didn't respond and she wasn't sure if he'd heard until she saw John at his doorway with a look of disbelief. "Seriously?"

Jenny chuckled. "Seriously."

"Damn that Dan. He is one lucky bugger." John disappeared back in his bedroom and started typing away.

She looked at the clock and realized Dan was over a half-hour late. She picked up her phone and called. It took several rings before he answered. "Hey, can't talk right now. Will call back as soon as I can. Order takeout for you and John. I will be a while."

Jenny could hear the stress in his voice. "What's going on, Dan?"

"Don't worry. I'm with Ryan."

"Do you want me to meet you?"

"No." He cleared his throat. "Sorry, he doesn't want you here. I'll explain things later, but I have to go." Jenny was shocked when he hung up on her.

Were the two going to duke it out again? Why would Dan go to Ryan again? It didn't make any sense, unless... *Kelly!*

It was excruciating to remain at John's apartment while she waited to find out the trouble Kelly had caused. Jenny paced the apartment, but couldn't find relief. She finally pulled out the paperwork for the rentals they were considering. There was a nice, but expensive, apartment not too far from John's place, a neglected house near Dan's work, and a modern townhome located on the outskirts of town. She was leaning towards the last one, but the drive would be annoying for them both. However, the price was right and it had an office and an extra bedroom for guests. The longer she considered the pluses and minuses of each, the more sure she felt about her initial choice. Dan had left the final decision to her, saying all three were equally viable.

Jenny needed to feel in control, so she called the landlord to inform him of her decision. That control was taken from her when he asked for her financial history. The minute she mentioned that she wasn't currently employed, he told her that he would have to talk to Dan. Jenny hung up, seething with anger. Kelly was *still* screwing with her life.

She began pacing again, wondering what the bitch had done to Ryan. When she couldn't stand it anymore, she burst into John's room and ranted. The poor man took it without complaint, but she noticed his look of relief when her phone rang.

"I'm on my way home and will give you all the details when I get there."

"Are you okay?"

"Yes."

"Is Ryan?"

Dan paused. "We'll talk about it when I get there."

As soon as Dan entered the apartment Jenny ran to his arms while checking for black eyes on his handsome face. Seeing none, she asked, "What happened? What did Kelly do?"

"She did the same thing to Ryan that she did to you. I never thought to warn him. I never considered she'd go after him like that…"

Jenny's hand flew to her mouth. "Oh no. Don't tell me she didn't distribute those damn photos."

"She did," Dan said, sounding drained. "We have been at the police station all night. You will need to go tomorrow."

Jenny collapsed on the couch. "Poor Rye. He didn't do anything to hurt her."

"It was a stab at you and me. Kelly doesn't care who gets harmed along the way."

She looked at him fearfully. "Did… Did Ryan lose his job?"

Dan actually smiled. "No, and you'll never guess who saved it."

"Who?"

"Remember his little temp? The one he complained about? According to Ryan, she may not file papers properly but she is a natural-born attorney. She argued for Ryan until his boss actually apologized to him. Ryan has never seen anything like it. No one wins an argument with his boss."

Jenny giggled in relief. "I can't imagine."

"Yeah, it's been a surreal day for Ryan, but he'll be all right."

"Dan…" Her lip quivered when she asked, "Did Ryan say why he didn't want me there?"

"I don't think you understand. The only reason he called me is that I'm his only friend and he was desperate. Ryan can't forgive you for leaving him."

It crushed her to know that they would never be friends again, but she understood. She'd hurt him in the deepest way possible. "Well, I'm glad he called you."

"Yeah, I'm glad, too. You should know that he filed charges against Kelly and expects you to do the same. He understands now that she played him. I think the full impact of her influence and the consequences of that are just now hitting him."

"Poor Rye. We didn't have to break up," she said woefully.

Dan cupped her chin. "As cruel as this sounds, I'm glad things fell apart. Now that I have had a chance to be with you exclusively, I can't imagine any other reality."

In her heart of hearts, Jenny agreed. She caressed his scruffy cheek. "Just you and me."

"Forever."

Winter Wedding

The morning of their wedding was a clear, sunny winter's day. The chill in the air and the snow on the ground were the only reminders of the season. The blue skies spoke to warmer times. "Looks like the perfect day, Dan," Jenny said, looking out the window. Unfortunately, he couldn't hear her. Her mom had insisted that she stay with them overnight to preserve the tradition of the groom not seeing the bride.

Her parents had flown in the day before and met Dan's parents for a formal dinner at an upscale restaurant paid for by his parents. It had been an unpleasant evening. Mrs. Hayes didn't talk much, but that didn't stop Jenny's dad from peppering her with questions. Neither set of parents were enthusiastic about the upcoming nuptials. It showed on their faces and in their conversations the entire evening. Jenny had looked over at Dan sadly several times during the meal, wishing things could be different.

But Dan had been sweet at the end of the evening. When they'd said good-bye she'd felt close to tears. He wiped the emerging tears away, whispering, "Only one more night." She'd nodded and quickly jumped into her father's car, afraid of losing her composure, but Dan motioned her to unroll the window. He'd brushed his hair back all cute-like before saying, "The next time we meet I will be saying 'I do'." He patted the car a couple of times and turned away. *Maybe it has been hard on him too...*

His words "I do" still rang in her head. A smile spread across her face as she stretched in the hotel bed. It was going to be a beautiful day and tonight she would be in Dan's arms—forever.

Jenny spent the morning primping. Her mother then helped her to style her hair, keeping it down and long, just the way Dan liked it. Her makeup was light and natural as well, honoring his simple tastes. When it came time to put on the dress, her mother unzipped the bag and carefully pulled out the gown.

Jenny stared at it in shock. "It's the wrong dress."

Her mother looked sick. "What do you mean it's the wrong dress? Oh my God, did the shopkeeper mix up your dress with another? What are we going to do?"

Jenny smiled with tears in her eyes. "Mom, it's not the dress I picked out. It's the dress of my dreams."

Her mother relaxed and brought the dress to

her. "You had me scared for a minute."

Jenny touched the lace and played with the buttons on the gown. "This gown cost a fortune, Mama. I can't believe Dan did this for me."

"It *is* exquisite, Jenny."

"I even checked it before I packed, just to make sure it wasn't wrinkled. I don't know how he did it, but I'm so thrilled he did!" She slipped it on and her mother helped with all the buttons. Both of them stared in the mirror, speechless. The lace, the row of buttons trailing up her back, and the way it hugged her curves made her feel elegant and sexy.

"Perfect," her mother sighed.

"Yes."

"But I think I have something that will make it even better. You need something blue, my darling." Her mother pulled out a black velvet box and handed it to her.

Jenny recognized the box. When she was a little girl she had often played with her mother's jewelry, but this was one piece she was not allowed to touch. "Oh, Mama…"

"It was the first piece of jewelry your father gave me. I've always loved it and now I want you to have it."

"I can't. Doda meant this for you."

"I talked to your father and he is in agreement. We both want you to have it. I wish we could give you more, darling. But times have been tough for your father the last few years. Just know this is given in love."

Jenny opened the box in awed reverence and looked at the diamond-encrusted sapphire. It was delicate and stunning. She took it out and handed it to her mother. Jenny closed her eyes as her mother clasped the necklace around her throat.

"Yes, it finishes the look," her mother said proudly, standing back and smiling. "You look so beautiful, Jenny. I don't think I have seen you this happy since you were a little girl."

"I am, Mama. I love Dan more than I can say."

"I had my doubts about his character, being Ryan's best friend, but his little surprise with the dress... well, I can't help seeing a bit of your father in him."

Jenny held back the tears as she hugged her mom. "It means the world to me that you can accept this wedding *and* him."

"I don't understand why you are rushing it, but knowing how I felt about your father when we first met, I believe time doesn't matter when it's right."

"Thank you, Mama."

"Darling, your happiness is my only concern." Her mother hugged her one last time, being exceedingly careful not to mess her dress and hair.

It was a long drive to the mountains, and although it was sunny in the city, the higher they went the cloudier the skies became. Jenny became concerned that the weather might ruin their wedding plans. *This is why outdoor weddings in the winter aren't done!* she scolded herself.

She was grateful when they made it to the wedding site and saw that everyone else had arrived. Her father helped her out of the car and held out his arm. Jenny took it gratefully, walking beside her father, bursting with joy as she gazed over the small gathering. She instantly recognized her future in-laws and Rose, but noticed a taller version of Dan standing next to a lanky blonde. She had to assume it was his brother Marcus because the guy looked just like Dan except for the dark hair.

Jenny's eyes naturally gravitated to her future husband. He was dangerously handsome in his tux, making her quiver inside. When he turned to face her and his whole face lit up, Jenny almost broke ranks and ran to him. It took great effort for her to remain by her father's side.

As she approached, Jenny tried to imagine what Dan was seeing—her long dark hair styled in loose ringlets, her stunning coat hugging the curves he loved so well, and the hint of her leather boots peeking out with each step. But he wasn't looking at any of those things; his eyes were locked on hers.

Dan stepped back as she came up beside him, giving her an unobstructed view of the person standing behind him. Jenny froze, unable to breathe.

Ryan nodded and said nonchalantly, "Hey, Jenny."

She was grateful for her father's supportive arm when her knees almost gave out. "Ryan, you're... here." Tears unwillingly formed.

He walked over to her, shaking his head. "No crying. I'll leave if you do."

She quickly wiped her eyes and smiled. However, her bottom lip quivered from the effort. "I didn't think…"

"Do you mind if I stand in as your maid of honor?" Ryan asked with a teasing smirk. "I heard you were lacking one."

"Really, Ryan? I…" A tear fell down her cheek.

"No crying, remember?" he said sternly. She nodded and bit her bottom lip to stop it from quivering.

"Let us proceed," stated an unfamiliar voice. Jenny looked up and saw the young pastor from the local mountain church was ready with his Bible clutched firmly in his hand.

Dan kissed her cheek. "Meet you out on the water, my little kumquat."

Jenny looked out over the pond and gasped. A long scarlet path lined with red and white poinsettias led out to the middle of the pond. At the end of the red path was a large arch cascading white flowers and red ribbons. Tall pines framed the icy pond as the large snowcapped peaks towered above.

A fairytale come to life… all but the gathering dark clouds. They looked suspiciously pregnant with snow. Jenny worried at the sudden drop in temperature as the winds began to gently swirl around them.

Rose handed her a bouquet of gardenias, tiny crimson roses, with a hint of pine interspersed with red and gold ribbon. A masterpiece in its own right.

"Thank you, Rose. This is exquisite."

"Only the best for you, sweetie. Knock 'em

dead." She swatted Jenny on the butt, and winked at Dan's mother, who stood several feet away looking serious and foreboding. Jenny turned away from Mrs. Hayes. She wasn't going to allow that woman's poor attitude to affect her wedding.

"It's time to make this official," her father announced in his low comforting voice, taking Jenny's hand back and giving it a fatherly pat.

She leaned her head against his strong shoulder. "Yes, Doda, let's."

The small wedding party gathered on the carpeted ice, leaving Jenny and her father behind. Her mother gave Jenny one last hug before taking her place. "I'm wishing you all my best, darling. Enjoy this moment, but know it only gets better from here."

Jenny looked out onto the pond, taking in the sight of Dan standing next to his older brother. Dan stood tall and confident, looking at her with a love that burned fiercely in its intensity.

As her father guided her on the red carpet, she glanced over at Ryan. His expression was one of tenderness. It both blessed and broke her heart. Ryan's presence was a gift beyond price.

Then Jenny locked eyes with Dan. His gaze was inviting, drawing her like a flame. *My husband...*

Everyone turned in response to the loud echoing roar of an engine. Jenny looked in the direction of the disturbance and gasped when she saw a red Camaro careening down the snowy path, fishtailing from side-to-side. "No!"

"It'll be all right, Jenny. Don't say anything, we've got this," Dan stated calmly.

Kelly jumped out of her car screaming, "Stop the wedding! Stop it right now! This woman is nothing but a whore. She's tricked Dan into marrying him. Everything she's said is nothing but lies!"

Both Dan and Ryan moved in unison, blocking Jenny from Kelly's wrath as she approached. "Turn around and go home. Now!" Dan ordered.

"No, I can't let you do this, Dan. It's a huge mistake." Kelly turned to Mrs. Hayes. "You're not going to allow this whore to marry your son, are you?"

Mrs. Hayes did not hesitate, stating coolly, "I believe my son told you to leave."

Kelly stared at her in disbelief. "Harriet, what are you saying? You know what she is. How can you take her side?"

Jenny's father growled, stepping towards Kelly threateningly. "I believe you were told to leave."

Kelly backed up, but looked around wildly until she spotted Ryan. "Come on! You can't let her get away with this. I thought you came to stop it, Ryan. Why would you condone her betrayal? What are you, some kind of fucking pussy?"

The lanky blonde hissed, "Watch what you say, you venomous…"

Marcus interrupted the exchange, stating loudly, "That's enough." He turned to Kelly, sounding suspiciously formal like a police officer. "I believe there is a restraining order against you." He walked up to her, taking something out of his pocket. Before Kelly knew what was happening, he'd handcuffed her wrist. "You are in violation of the law. You can go quietly or additional charges will be filed against you." He walked her to his car and called out to Dan, "I'll be back in a minute."

He drove the car to an alcove of pine trees and got out, walking back to the group. "She's handcuffed to the seat. That should keep her quiet while we get on with the happy event."

Jenny's parents looked at their daughter questioningly, unaware of the trouble Kelly had caused them.

Jenny was unsure where to begin and was relieved when Mrs. Hayes answered for her. "Kelly is still struggling with their decision, but I trust she will get over it. We anticipated she might be a problem today, which is why I asked my son Marcus to bring his handcuffs."

As much as Harriet didn't want the marriage to take place, she had taken precautions to protect the ceremony. Jenny was shocked and mouthed the words, "Thank you," to her. The woman met her appreciation with a cold stare, but nodded stiffly.

The small group took their places again and the pastor began the ceremony. "Dearly beloved, we are gathered here…" Jenny was barely aware of his words the moment Dan took her hands in his. Dan must have noticed her delirium, because he gently squeezed her hand and she heard the words, "… say I do."

Jenny giggled nervously, embarrassed she'd almost missed her cue. "I do. I most definitely do."

The pastor continued on, but her heart was beating so loudly by then that it drowned out his words. She saw Dan's perfect lips form the words "I do" and her whole body broke out in a warm flush.

"The couple has chosen to share their own vows during the exchange of rings."

Jenny pulled off her glove and handed it to Ryan. She smiled bashfully when Dan took her left hand in his. He slipped his great-grandmother's wedding band on her finger and then brought her hand to his lips. The love reflected in his eyes melted her heart.

"Jenny, my life didn't start until I met you. Everything before was just going through the motions, but I didn't know it. I was blind until you came into my life and gave it color. I love everything about you, from this long beautiful hair," he said, playing with a dark curl, "to this gorgeous Cherokee skin." He caressed her cheek lightly. "But it is your adventurous spirit I admire most. I feel like… No, I *am* the luckiest man on the planet." He took her other hand and squeezed both tightly. "You are my treasure and I will endeavor to remind you of that every day." He gave her a little wink when he added, "It will be my pleasure to do so."

Marcus handed her Dan's ring. Jenny's hands trembled slightly as she guided the gold band onto his finger. She took a deep breath, wanting to drink in the moment a little longer.

"Dan, I have finally found myself in you. Your love complements me." She inadvertently glanced at the edge of the pond, remembering their last visit to this place. Dan responded with a low chuckle, letting her know he was thinking of the same memory. "You seem to understand me on a level no one else does. Your wisdom, patience, and love have transformed me into someone new. I can't imagine life without you now." She looked deeply into Dan's brown eyes and smiled. "Dan William Hayes, I pledge my loyalty and love to you and I cannot wait to share the rest of my life's journey with you by my side." Jenny went to kiss him, but remembered halfway and stopped herself.

Several people laughed when the pastor cautioned her, "Now, now… no need to rush." He then announced in a dramatic voice loud enough to echo off the snowcapped peaks, "What God has joined together, let no man put asunder!" When the muted echoes died off, he added in a tender tone, "And so, by the power vested in me, I now pronounce you man and wife." He grinned at the groom. "You may now kiss the eager bride."

Dan put his hands around Jenny's waist and tilted his head slightly as he went in for the kiss. It started off tender, but then he parted her lips with his tongue and took his bride. Marcus cleared his throat, bringing them both back to reality. Dan broke the embrace and they looked at each other and laughed.

The pastor didn't miss a beat. "I present to you,

Mr. and Mrs. Dan Hayes."

Dan took Jenny's hand and they faced the small group. Her heart felt close to bursting as she walked back down the red carpet as the new Mrs. Hayes.

Dan's parents made it a point to congratulate them first. Mr. Hayes hugged his son, thumping him hard on the back. "You've taken on quite a responsibility. Don't you dare fail your new wife."

"I only learned from the best, Pops. No worries there."

Mr. Hayes turned to Jenny. "You are officially my daughter now. I've never had one before, but I'll do my best to do right by you." He took Jenny in his arms and gave her a real hug. She sighed inwardly, happy to receive his love.

"Thank you… Dad." It felt a little weird saying it, especially with her father standing close by, but Jenny couldn't have been happier.

"Yes, welcome to our family. I hope you enjoy our honeymoon gift," Mrs. Hayes stated with exaggerated formality. She did not make a move to hug Jenny.

"I'm sure I will."

Dan's father took a key from his pocket with a red bow attached and handed it to her. "From our family to your new family."

Jenny took the key as Dan put his arm around her. "It's the cabin."

Mr. Hayes explained, "Harriet and I both felt it was the perfect gift for you two. I am sure Gammy and Poppy would approve."

Jenny studied Dan's mother carefully. "Are you sure, Mrs. Hayes?"

"It's 'mother' to you."

Jenny gave a spontaneous hug to the stiff woman. "Thanks, Mom!"

Dan joined in the hug, forcing Harriet to respond to the group embrace. She sputtered, "That's quite enough, you two." She straightened her jacket before adding, "I made a few changes to one of the rooms. I hope it will be suitable."

Jenny threatened to hug her again, so she quickly stepped backwards to get away from Jenny's reach and bumped into Ryan. Poor Mrs. Hayes looked mortified and made an abrupt beeline for the pastor.

Ryan looked at Jenny and Dan awkwardly. "Sorry, but I didn't bring a gift."

Jenny gushed, "Rye, coming today was the greatest gift you could give!"

He nodded towards the lanky blonde with short, bobbed hair standing a few feet away. "It's Roxanne's fault. She said I would regret it later if I didn't come." Jenny looked at the woman with renewed interest, realizing she was Marcus' date after all. The woman was attractive—tall, blonde, the exact opposite of Jenny.

Ryan explained, "She's my temp."

"Oh, the attorney in disguise," Jenny acknowledged. "She *must* be good at the powers of persuasion to get you to come today."

Ryan gazed at Roxanne with admiration. "Yeah, she's a smart lady and she's right. I still care about you and Dan… despite everything."

"I'm glad to hear it, Rye," Jenny said, tentatively reaching out to give him a hug. He tensed and she stepped back in response, suddenly aware of the nerves he was trying to hide. She smiled, hoping to express her heart without bringing him further pain. "Ryan, you being here is the best gift ever." She swallowed back the lump in her throat, adding, "I will hold this memory dear to me always."

Ryan's lips twitched and he looked desperately at Roxanne for support. She walked over to him and broke the awkward silence that hung in the mountain air. "I am glad I was able to attend your wedding, Mrs. Hayes. Getting to meet you gives me a better idea who Ryan is."

Jenny was concerned for Ryan's well-being, so she cut their conversation short. "I know you two have a long drive back. I thank you for coming—for everything."

Dan shook Ryan's hand and said gruffly, "Thank you, Ryan."

Ryan responded with a hard handshake. His voice faltered when he replied, "Take care of her." He immediately took Roxanne's hand and headed towards their car just as the snow began to fall.

Jenny's mom came up and wrapped her in a hug, distracting Jenny from the poignant scene. "It was a lovely wedding and the vows you shared were beautiful." She grabbed onto Dan and squeezed him, too. "I have a good feeling about you both." She nudged him playfully. "And that dress stunt you pulled on my daughter made me a fan forever."

Dan brushed back his hair, obviously embarrassed by her praise. "I love your daughter, Mrs. Cole."

Her father put his sizeable hand on Dan's shoulder. "We believe that. My only advice is to be honest and respectful of each other. You can work through most anything if you remember that."

"Sound advice, sir."

The snow was coming down with greater intensity. Dan pulled Jenny's hood around her face and patted her on the head. The flakes were small, but they were increasing in number, making visibility an issue.

"Looks like it's going to be a bad storm," Marcus announced. The newlyweds smiled at each other.

Dan told him, "That it does. You better get crazy woman out of here before she kills herself on the road."

Marcus chuckled, "Don't worry, I will be following her all the way down. There is no way she will escape my watchful eye."

"Thanks, brother."

Marcus turned to Jenny and picked her up without warning. He hugged her in midair, squeezing the breath out of her. "Welcome to the Hayes clan, sis. I'll have to get some alone time with you so I can share Dan's darkest and most embarrassing moments." She giggled when he put her down. The similarities between the two were disconcerting and made her feel slightly giddy.

The wedding party quickly broke up as people rushed to beat the worst of the storm. Everyone except for the newlyweds, who headed directly to the cabin. When they arrived, Dan insisted on carrying Jenny over the threshold. He unlocked the door and turned on the light before coming back for her.

Dan brushed the snow off her hood. "You officially look like a snow princess." He kissed her cold lips and smiled. "My personal snow princess..." He picked her up and kissed her again as he carried her through the doorway. The warmth of the cabin embraced her as they entered. Dan broke the kiss and put her down slowly before saying, "Oh shit."

Jenny stared at the elegantly set table complete with candles and wine. The oven was on warm and she deduced a lovely dinner was waiting for them. "Did your mother do this?" she asked in surprise.

"It does seem like her handiwork," he said wearily.

"But she's opposed to our marriage."

Dan looked apologetic when he said, "Baby, there is one thing you have to know about my mother, she is all about appearance. She wouldn't want anyone to accuse her of being cheap or uncaring." He hugged her to his chest. "This is more about making herself feel better than it is about us."

"That's too bad," she said, frowning.

"Don't take it personally. My mother still has a

lot of growing up to do." He walked over to the table and lifted a napkin off one of the dishes, taking a roll for himself and handing her one.

Jenny was starving and took a bite of the yeasty bread, deciding to accept the gift for what it was. "So your mom said that she changed one of the rooms, right? Do you think this is what she meant?"

"Knowing my mother, I would say no."

Jenny's face lit up and she raced to the nearest bedroom. It was still the same cold room she had tried to sleep in during the blizzard. She moved on to the second bedroom—the one where they had first snuggled together and later expressed deeper feelings for one another. *If his mother only knew...*

She squealed in delight when she saw how Mrs. Hayes had transformed it from a simple cabin room to a luxurious love nest in browns and maroons. A large four-poster queen bed filled the small space and the windows were covered in rich decorative curtains, helping to keep in the warmth. The old chest at the foot of the bed had been replaced with a stylish one made of hardwood and there was an antique self-standing mirror tucked in the corner. Dan seemed intrigued by the piece.

Jenny asked, "How did she know this room is special to us, Dan? You didn't tell her, did you?"

He chuckled, pulling her to him. "No. This used to be Gammy and Poppy's room."

Jenny looked down at her wedding set and smiled, overwhelmed by the connection she felt with his great-grandmother. She was certain that

Gammy would approve of their union.

"My love, I think it is time I take off this coat and see the beautiful bride underneath." Dan undid the big buttons one by one before slipping it off her shoulders. "Oh yes, as lovely as I remember."

Jenny threw her arms around him. "I can't believe you got me the dress, Dan. Why would you do that? I'm the only one who gets to enjoy it."

"Not true. I did it for purely selfish reasons. It was the dress I wanted my bride wrapped in." He smiled, looking down at her tenderly. "Besides, I did not buy you a ring. You deserved it." Dan took her hand and twirled her around twice as he looked over the gown. "You have never looked more beautiful to me than you do right now, wife."

Jenny felt butterflies when he called her 'wife'. "Thank you, husband."

"Whoa, that's weird hearing you say that." He leaned in next to her ear. "But I like it." Shivers ran down her spine as he kissed her neck. "My wife, to have and to hold…" He wrapped his arms around her and continued to kiss and nibble.

"Dan, I feel like I am going to melt when you do that."

He held her tighter, biting her neck and murmuring, "Melt into me, wife."

Jenny obeyed and laid her head against his chest, giving into the fire he was fanning. His strong hands explored the lace of her dress, concentrating on the hardness of her nipples. She moaned, feeling her loins contract in pleasure from his attention.

"Shall I undress you or let you remain in your bridal gown a little longer?"

"Undress me."

He chuckled. "I think you are too beautiful to unwrap just yet."

She groaned. Dan let go of her and left the room. She reluctantly followed him out and watched him build a fire in the fireplace. He looked up after he got the fire going and said with a grin, "Just in case the power goes out again."

"I wonder if your mom bought Vienna sausages and Pop-Tarts in case of power failure," she joked.

"Let's check." The two opened the cupboards and saw they'd been stocked with all kinds of staples, but zero convenience foods.

"I suppose we could live on handfuls of flour," he commented.

"Should we eat your mother's meal? I'm starving!"

He cleared his throat. "Baby, I hate to tell you this but it's going to be lamb."

"Lamb? But I don't eat innocent babies…"

He patted her head. "I know. But you see, my mother is convinced that any major celebration includes lamb. It should make future holidays with my family loads of fun."

"Dan. I really want your mom to accept me." She sighed and looked at him sadly. "Should I force myself to eat lamb?"

He put his hands around her waist and smiled. "Don't compromise who you are. She will learn to love you, trust me." He opened the fridge and pulled out a large white box. "So no baby animals, but maybe I can interest you in cake."

Dan carefully took the cake out and placed it on the table. It was exquisite with the realistic flowers and delicate floating butterflies—the exact opposite of the weather raging outside.

"Just looking at it makes me happy!" Jenny smiled.

"Wait until you taste it," he said hungrily, pulling a knife out of the drawer.

She put her hands over the cake to protect it. "No! You can't cut this beautiful piece of art."

"The cake was made to be eaten, woman. The Trans will be upset if we don't eat the cake that they handmade with love. You don't want to reject their love, do you?"

Jenny rolled her eyes. "Man, you're laying it on thick."

"I'm hungry," he complained, his stomach growling in agreement. "So can I cut the cake now?"

She didn't answer him right away, putting her hand over his instead. "Let's cut it together." Jenny helped him slice through the confection, cutting out two small pieces.

He handed her one and he took the other. "Keeping with tradition, I think we should feed each other."

"No smashing it in my face, Dan," she warned.

He looked crushed. "As if I would ever do that to the woman I love."

Jenny hesitantly brought the cake to his lips as his piece moved closer to her face.

"You don't trust me," he accused.

She giggled. "Not completely."

"Tsk, tsk, wife. This is not how a stable marriage starts off."

"You're just trying to distract me," she said, ready to smash the cake in his face the minute he made his move.

"Open your mouth and close your eyes, Jenny."

She shook her head. "No way am I going to be a sitting duck for you."

He commanded in a quiet but firm tone, "Do it, my love."

She could tell he was taking it more seriously than she was, so she kept her cake positioned next to his face as she cautiously closed her eyes. Jenny parted her lips and he gently brought the wedding cake to her mouth, allowing her to take a small bite. The flavors that flooded her tastebuds reminded her of the sweet flowers of spring and she moaned in pleasure. Jenny cracked an eye open.

"Now do you trust me?"

"Yes," she answered sheepishly. Jenny held the cake up to him and watched her handsome groom take the bite she offered.

He smiled appreciatively while he chewed. "The Trans make a damn fine cake."

"Yes, they do," she answered as she took a scoop of icing and wiped it on his nose.

"You didn't."

She couldn't help laughing at how ridiculous he looked. He returned the favor by icing her chin and then commanded, "Lick it off me, woman."

She dutifully licked his nose as he licked off the icing on her chin. The licks soon gravitated to the middle and the kisses became passionate. Jenny crawled onto his lap as they gave into their mutual lust.

Dan finally broke the embrace, his manhood making his state of arousal quite obvious. "Before we retire to the bedroom, there is one more tradition I would like to observe. I want to see you dance in this lovely dress before I peel it off."

His compliment pleased her and she eagerly took the hand he offered her. Dan led her to the middle of the room and then went over to the stereo to pick out a song. Jenny stood quietly, staring at the fireplace, appreciating how fervently the flames consumed the wood. *Dan—the flame that consumes me...*

He turned off the lights and the cabin was bathed in the romantic glow of the fire. He motioned her to him. "Come, wife."

The sad melodic beginning of Blue October's *Congratulations* drifted through air, harmonizing with the lonely sound of the wind raging outside. Dan took her right hand in his left and settled his right hand in the small of her back. He guided Jenny around the room, speaking softly to her. "When you played this song that first night, I thought my heart would break. I wanted to tell you how I felt, but I couldn't bring myself to ruin what we already had. That night, I had pretty much resigned myself to the fact I would end up like the guy in the song. Standing by, watching you marry Ryan."

"You were so discreet about your feelings, Dan. I never knew."

"If it hadn't been for that blessed snowstorm, I don't think I ever would have been honest with you."

Jenny laid her head on his chest and sighed contentedly. "I'm so glad you were... *husband.*"

When the song ended, he twirled her around once watching the sway of her gown. She loved how he made her feel so special, so incredibly treasured.

"Dan, as sweet as it is to walk down memory lane, I believe we need to dance to a different song on our wedding day." She walked over to the stereo, knowing the exact song she wanted. "As you know, Blue October has very few upbeat, happy songs, but I think this one will do." Jenny hit the play button and walked back to Dan swaying to Justin's voice singing *a cappella.*

Dan instantly smiled. "Ah yes, *Calling You.* The perfect song." He took her in his arms again and they danced around the room to the livelier beat, singing the words while they looked into each other's eyes. At the end of the song, they broke apart and made fools of themselves as the two danced to Justin's "oh, wo, oh, oh, oh's".

When the music faded, Dan smiled. "I know what I want now." He left her standing alone as he went to the bedroom. He came back out carrying the full-length mirror and placed it in the middle of the room. "Stand in front of it, Jenny."

He moved behind her and looked at her lustfully through the reflection in the mirror. His face glowed in the firelight, giving him an ominous, sexy look. With slow, delicious diligence he unbuttoned her gown while she watched. "I figured you should see the beauty I see."

Jenny watched with heady anticipation as the dress slowly loosened with each button. He slipped the lace material from her shoulders and kissed them.

She moaned and turned her head to kiss him back, but he said, "No, Jenny, remain still and watch your undressing." He continued one by one, undoing each button until the bodice fell to her waist.

Dan unhooked her bra and let it fall to the floor, then he wrapped his strong hands around each full breast and squeezed. "So damn sexy, I am sorely tempted to make love to them with my cock."

Jenny smiled. "I think you need to unbutton a little further."

He nibbled her ear and growled, "I'll save that for later then." The gown finally slipped from her waist and pooled at her feet, leaving her with only her garters and lace panties. "Oh Jenny," he groaned, running his hands over her copper skin.

She tilted her head back against his broad chest and let him have his way with her. One set of fingers teased her nipples while the other slipped under her panties and explored her pussy. Jenny squirmed against him, loving the way he played her body.

Dan slipped his middle finger into her depths and began rubbing against her clit. Each pass tugged on the hood, sending bursts of electricity to her groin. "I want you to look into the mirror as you come, Jenny. I want you to see what I see."

Jenny watched as his hand made love to her. She bit her lip and moaned, tilting her head back as her back instinctively arched against him.

"No, baby. Watch…"

She looked at the mirror again, but she was finding it difficult to stand as her body tensed in expectancy of its release. "Hold me," she begged. He stopped playing with her breasts and wrapped one arm around her as support while the other continued its relentless teasing.

Jenny's eyes glazed over with lust as the tension increased. She watched her nipples get rock hard as a rose-colored blush took over her chest. She was dangerously close, just one more pass…

She became silent. Her muscles tensed as she crested the peak and her pussy began dancing rhythmically around his middle finger. Jenny whimpered, her body enthusiastically squeezing Dan's finger in its blind adoration of him.

"Do you see how beautiful you are when you come?" he whispered.

She gazed into the mirror but her eyes were

locked on his, which added to the intensity of the moment. Jenny moaned softly and collapsed in his arms. He pulled his finger from her and held her for several moments, crooning, "My wife, my beautiful wife…" He then picked her up and carried her to the bedroom.

"Now to make love to you properly."

When he placed her on the bed, Jenny rolled over and got on all fours. "Not before I love your husbandly cock with my mouth."

Dan smiled, shedding his clothes—taking his sweet time to rid himself of the jacket, gold vest, red tie, white shirt, pants and boxers. She trembled as she watched the private strip show. She took in the manliness of his shaft—thick, hard, surrounded in handsome blond curls.

Jenny leaned over and took the first tentative lick, catching the drop of precome dripping from his shaft. She heard his intake of breath and smiled. Jenny stuck her ass in the air teasingly as she wrapped her hand around the base and began stroking his rigid member. She added the swirling of her tongue over the head, delighting in his cock—warm, smooth, with a sensitive ridge to torment and tease.

"Jenny… baby… stop," he gasped.

She sucked even harder as she increased the pace of her stroke. More precome greeted her tongue, warning her that he was close, but she couldn't stop. She *needed* to taste his essence.

Two firm hands grabbed her shoulders and

pulled her from his shaft.

"No," she protested.

"I don't think you understand, my bride. This cock is coming inside you tonight, not down your throat." With that, he flipped her onto her back, ripped off her panties and positioned himself between her legs.

"Not fair!" she protested.

Dan didn't answer as he plunged his shaft inside her. Jenny cried out at the depth of his thrust. "Oh my God, you're so deep!"

Dan growled, "I've been holding back until now." He grabbed her shoulders and began thrusting at a depth and rate she hadn't experienced before. Jenny opened and shut her mouth in silent screams of pleasure. When he stopped to catch his breath, her body caught up and came around his shaft shamelessly.

He smiled down at her. "Number two."

Dan then lifted her legs straight in the air and closed them together, blocking her view of him. The thrusting started up again, sending her pussy into quivering spasms. He stopped and dropped her legs. Dan moved between her thighs, rubbing her clit with his long, rolling pelvic thrusts.

Jenny thrashed her head back and forth, completely entranced by his taking of her. Each roll of his hips brushed his groin against her clit, sending flames to her core. He stopped again and grabbed her face in his hands, kissing her deeply, exploring the recesses of her mouth as her body tensed a third time and began contracting around his shaft. He groaned into her mouth as his cock pulsated in release, covering her insides with his love.

Jenny wrapped her legs around him, moaning with unrestrained passion. When his shaft was finally spent, Dan rolled next to her and let out a long sigh of satisfaction.

"I've been waiting to do that for a long time."

Jenny propped her head with her hand and grinned. "What? Make me come three times?"

He turned his head towards her, his bangs flirtatiously covering his eyes. "No. Giving you all of me."

His answer thrilled her. Jenny brushed back his blond hair with her fingers, looking into those dark brown eyes. "All this time, I never suspected…"

"I'm full of all kinds of surprises, little wife."

Jenny smiled seductively. "You're not the only one, husband. Wait here." Jenny got up and headed for the kitchen. She grabbed a bowl from under the counter, trying to be quiet as to not raise suspicion. She held her breath before opening the outside door and quickly scooping a generous helping of snow from the drift next to the cabin. She shivered as she shut the door against the wind. It was seriously picking up, leaving her with no doubt they would be snowed in by morning.

"What are you doing out there, Jenny?" he called from the bedroom.

"Just checking the storm. Looks like it is going to be a doozie. But don't you worry, honey. Your little wifey is getting your surprise ready as we speak." Jenny fashioned a large donut out of snow, one with a hole just big enough to fit around a certain part of Dan's anatomy.

She placed it back in the bowl and sauntered to the bedroom with a wicked little grin. "So Dan, have you ever…"

WHAT TO READ NEXT

You can begin the journey into the sensual world of BDSM with the popular

Box Set of *Brie's Submission* – which is FREE!

Start reading NOW

Reviews mean the world to me!

I truly appreciate you taking the time to review ***Blissfully Undone***.

If you could leave a review on both Goodreads and the site where you purchased this eBook from, I would be so grateful. Sincerely, ~Red

ABOUT THE AUTHOR

Over Two Million readers have enjoyed
Red's stories

Red Phoenix – USA Today Bestselling Author
Winner of 8 Readers' Choice Awards

Hey Everyone!

I'm Red Phoenix, an author who also happens to be
a submissive in real life. I wrote the Brie's
Submission series because I wanted people
everywhere to know just how much fun BDSM
can be.

There is a huge cast of characters who are part of
Brie's journey. The further you read into the story
the more you learn about each one. I hope you grow
to love Brie and the gang as much as I do.

They've become like family.

When I'm not writing, you can find me online
with readers.

I heart my fans! ~Red

To find out more visit my Website

redphoenixauthor.com

Follow Me on BookBub

bookbub.com/authors/red-phoenix

Newsletter: Sign up

redphoenixauthor.com/newsletter-signup

Facebook: RedPhoenix69

Twitter: @redphoenix69

Instagram: RedPhoenixAuthor

I invite you to join my reader Group!

facebook.com/groups/539875076052037

SIGN UP FOR MY NEWSLETTER
HERE FOR THE LATEST RED
PHOENIX UPDATES

SALES, GIVEAWAYS, NEW
RELEASES, EXCLUSIVE SNEAK
PEEKS, AND MORE!

SIGN UP HERE

REDPHOENIXAUTHOR.COM/
NEWSLETTER-SIGNUP

Red Phoenix is the author of:

Brie's Submission Series:

***You can also purchase the
AUDIO BOOK Versions**

Also part of the Submissive Training Center world:

Other Books by Red Phoenix

His Scottish Pet: Dom of the Ages
* Available in eBook and paperback

Audio Book: *His Scottish Pet: Dom of the Ages*

(Scottish Dom—A sexy Dom escapes to Scotland in the late 1400s. He encounters a waif who has the potential to free him from his tragic curse)

The Erotic Love Story of Amy and Troy
* Available in eBook and paperback

(Sexual Adventures—True love reigns, but fate continually throws Troy and Amy into the arms of others)

eBooks

Varick: The Reckoning

(Savory Vampire—A dark, sexy vampire story. The hero navigates the dangerous world he has been thrust into with lusty passion and a pure heart)

Keeper of the Wolf Clan (Keeper of Wolves, #1)

(Sexual Secrets—A virginal werewolf must act as the clan's mysterious Keeper)

The Keeper Finds Her Mate (Keeper of Wolves, #2)

(Second Chances—A young she-wolf must choose between old ties or new beginnings)

The Keeper Unites the Alphas (Keeper of Wolves, #3)

(Serious Consequences—The young she-wolf is captured by the rival clan)

Boxed Set: Keeper of Wolves Series (Books 1-3)

(Surprising Secrets—A secret so shocking it will rock Layla's world. The young she-wolf is put in a position of being able to save her werewolf clan or becoming the reason for its destruction)

Socrates Inspires Cherry to Blossom

(Satisfying Surrender—A mature and curvaceous woman becomes fascinated by an online Dom who has much to teach her)

By the Light of the Scottish Moon

(Saving Love—Two lost souls, the Moon, a
werewolf, and a death wish…)

In 9 Days

(Sweet Romance—A young girl falls in love with the
new student, nicknamed "the Freak")

---

9 Days and Counting

(Sacrificial Love—The sequel to *In 9 Days* delves
into the emotional reunion of two longtime lovers)

And Then He Saved Me

(Saving Tenderness—When a young girl tries to kill
herself, a man of great character intervenes with a
love that heals)

Play With Me at Noon

(Seeking Fulfillment—A desperate wife lives out her
fantasies by taking five different men in five days)

Connect with Red on Substance B

Substance B is a platform for independent authors to directly connect with their readers. Please visit Red's Substance B page where you can:

- Sign up for Red's newsletter
- Send a message to Red
- See all platforms where Red's books are sold

Visit Substance B today to learn more about your favorite independent authors.

Made in the USA
Coppell, TX
27 January 2022

72482628R00164